Praise for Avery Beck's *Sexy by Design*

"Erotic tantalizing passion!"

~ *Tulip, Whipped Cream Reviews*

"I was very pleased with this story and will look for author Beck's works in the future. ...it was packed with a whole lot of internal conflicts, drama, humor and hot scenes. The thrill of the chase and discovery are key elements that make this tale memorable. Also, just when I began to think that all the bases were covered a new twist would present itself and keep the pages turning."

~ *Natalie, www.ireadromance.com*

Sexy by Design

Avery Beck

A Samhain Publishing, Ltd. publication.

Samhain Publishing, Ltd.
577 Mulberry Street, Suite 1520
Macon, GA 31201
www.samhainpublishing.com

Sexy by Design
Copyright © 2010 by Avery Beck
Print ISBN: 978-1-60504-561-0
Digital ISBN: 978-1-60504-538-2

Editing by Tera Kleinfelter
Cover by Natalie Winters

First Samhain Publishing, Ltd. electronic publication: May 2009
First Samhain Publishing, Ltd. print publication: March 2010

Dedication

For Vicki, who introduced me to romance novels when she gave me a stack I couldn't put down—I know it isn't coincidence that my first published book released this May. We miss you.

Editor Tera—thanks for making the dream a reality!

Chapter One

The bright orange chunk of silicone looked like something that belonged on the street barricading road work rather than an item meant to end up between a woman's legs. Bree suspected, though, that comparing a vibrator to a traffic cone wouldn't persuade many customers of its pleasure-inducing capabilities.

She tore her attention away from the toy and turned back to the cursor on her screen. She had little time and a lot of white space to fill with a dazzling overview of her boss's latest novelty.

"Hey, Big B!"

The company's art director blew into her office and thrust a sheet of paper in her face. "Here's the final artwork for the new product page. Pretty nice, eh?"

Bree snatched the document from Todd's hand while he made himself comfortable on the edge of her desk. If she didn't like him so much, she'd never let him get away with that nickname, despite the knowledge that it referred to her height rather than the figure she worked hard to maintain. At five feet, ten inches, she towered above the other women in the office. It was one more way she didn't quite fit in at Paula's Pleasure House.

At least her genetic make up was out of her control, and no one could fault her for that. Not the way they could for, say, being a near-virgin in a company full of brazen extroverts who discussed their intimate adventures around the water cooler. Luckily, her colleagues didn't have any idea that the raciest parts of her sexual history were the short, tight clothes she'd bought specifically for this job.

"Wow." She gaped at the provocative image on the paper before handing it back to Todd. "That looks fun."

"You're telling me. I can hardly wait to take home the new stuff every month. Good thing we get an employee discount." He grinned, his eyebrows wiggling above his black-rimmed glasses.

Bree laughed in spite of the envy that zinged through her chest. She could only dream of having a permanent partner to share the inventory with. "Maybe you and Sasha should join the product testing team."

His smile wavered at the mention of his wife. He hopped off the desk. "Now there's an idea. The graphic file's in the usual place on the server. Let me know if you have any problems with it."

"Thanks." She watched his bleached hair disappear down the hallway, hoping the couple hadn't had an argument. Her feelings toward Todd ended at good friend and marketing cohort, but she'd give her eyeteeth and just about anything else to enjoy the romantic, spicy marriage he and Sasha had known for twelve years. At the rate she was going, she'd be lucky to experience a marriage at all.

Determined to keep her mind on the job, she opened the graphic. It portrayed a gorgeous blonde submerged in a hot tub, her head thrown back in ecstasy. A muscular man pressed her against the side of the tub, his arms strategically positioned so customers could imagine the gratifying ways he might be using the featured product below the surface of the water. Despite the chill of the air-conditioned building, beads of sweat broke out on Bree's forehead.

She took great pride in her post as web designer for Paula's Pleasure House, an online store offering everything from handcuffs to lingerie and anything else that catered to couples' fantasies. Lively, pink-haired Paula Willett had founded the thriving company, which had been serving Silicon Valley and the rest of the sexually curious nation for ten years. It was a lot more exciting than the cubicle-dwelling IT job Bree had left a few months ago—she just wished she could experience some of the excitement firsthand.

The picture on her monitor, for instance. That looked well worth a try.

"Okay, let's do this." Releasing a slow breath, she closed the file and looked again at the product that lay on her desk next to her favorite photo of her golden retriever. A glittery sticker on the package boasted that anyone who ordered the three-speed waterproof toy this week would receive a *free bath pillow!*

She smiled and shook her head, not sure which fascinated her more—the fact that Paula sold such kinky items, or the number of people who bought them.

She positioned her fingers over the keyboard and typed a few words. Neglected parts of her body came to life when she imagined the new experiences she could encourage her customers to enjoy. *Water's for More Than Washing With the New—*

"Breeee!" Paula rushed down the hall, then came to an abrupt stop in the doorway. "Lordy, Lordy...Bree."

She bent to catch her breath. Her low-cut top fell forward and revealed a lacy neon bra that matched her tinted hair. Bree glanced down at her own outfit, a simple black dress with spaghetti straps. She'd felt naked trying it on in the dressing room, but it looked conservative next to Paula's getup. All those years of being taught that "proper ladies don't bare their shoulders" had really messed with her fashion sense. Not to mention her sex life.

Paula stood back up, brandishing a stack of paperwork and a hopeful expression. "Do you have the page done for the Bath Buddy yet?"

"Not quite. I plan to have it ready by the end of the day." She hoped her face didn't give away the fact that she had written only eight words.

"Please do. The page *has* to be up tomorrow morning for this month's promotion, or else I'd give you another day. I know the schedule's been tight. I don't suppose there's any way you can stay late?"

"Paula, of course I can, but I really think I'll finish it by—"

"Oh, good, because I'm going to have to pass these on to you." She dropped the papers onto Bree's desk with a thud. "There's a meeting in ten minutes I cannot miss, and I have a feeling it will go well into the afternoon and I have to pick up my little brother from the airport and I don't know how I'll fit in..."

As Paula chattered on, Bree's focus shifted to the invoices that loomed in front of her, casting a shadow over the ever more intriguing Bath Buddy. On slow days she had no problem helping Paula with overflowing workloads, but she was pushing her deadline already. That pile looked like a half-day's worth of work. If she took it on, she would never finish the web page in time for its unveiling in the morning.

"Actually I—wait a minute. I pass by the airport on my way home. I can get your brother if you need to stay here."

Please say yes. She didn't exactly live next door to the airport, but she would much rather drive a few minutes out of her way to pick up the kid than risk missing the most important deadline of the month.

The six-month contract she'd signed with the company would end in three short weeks unless Paula agreed to make her a permanent hire. Every move Bree made was probably being scrutinized, and she would do whatever it took to keep her position. She loved this job and the way it defined her new, adventurous persona. For the first time in her life, she was happy, and she had no intention of going back to the way things used to be.

Paula chewed on a pen. "You know, that's not a bad idea. I can handle this paperwork after my meeting if I don't have to leave."

"It's no problem at all. What time does the flight come in?"

"I'll get you a copy of the itinerary. I always meet him at the coffee shop on the first floor. He's a real tall guy, dark hair..." She picked up the invoices and lugged them out the door, still mumbling.

Laughing quietly at Paula's endless supply of energy, Bree turned back to the computer. *You'll Be Breathless When You Dive In With The Bath Buddy AquaPleaser.*

Jessica would love it. A regular customer of Paula's Pleasure House—or PPH as it was known among the employees—she had been the one to notice the open webmaster position and suggest that Bree put her business degree to more exotic use.

"Oh—Jess!" Recalling their plans for the evening, she grabbed the phone and punched in her friend's work number.

"Smith, Kody, Silverman and Blanch, this is Jessica Winter speaking."

"You're like a terrible porn movie. Paralegal by day, harlot by night."

"Girl, you're not kidding!" Jess giggled, abandoning her professional demeanor at the sound of Bree's voice. "But hey, my dates thoroughly enjoy it when I play the naughty legal secretary. Many thanks to you."

"Yeah. Too bad I don't get to benefit from all the orders I've placed here." To take advantage of her twenty percent discount,

Bree purchased Jessica's items on her credit card in return for cash upon delivery.

"That's your own fault. There's a plethora of men at Barry's just waiting to get into your pants."

"Jessie!"

"It's true."

She shivered at the memory of the night her ex-boyfriend's betrayal had driven her into the bed of a complete stranger—and she'd been clueless as to what to do with him. "I don't care. We all know how well that turned out last time."

"Phooey on last time. Give it another chance."

"No way. I'm just calling to see if we can push our workout time back. I need to run an errand for my boss."

"Fine, change the subject," Jessica huffed. "What time do you want to meet?"

"Eight-ish?"

"Great. See you at the gym."

"Bye, Jess." She hung up quickly to avoid another discussion about the so-called joys of picking up anonymous guys in bars. Jessica relentlessly tried to push her back into the dating game, and Bree couldn't make her understand that she didn't want to play.

She ran her finger across the glass of her dog's picture frame. "I'm afraid it's going to be you and me for a while, Ginger."

She and Ginger had lived alone since the day a positive pregnancy test appeared in the bathroom trash. Given the three years she had shared with Jeff and the ring she'd anticipated every Christmas—and every Valentine's Day, and each birthday—the sight would have made her feel warm and fuzzy if she hadn't been on the Pill, and her period to boot.

Her gut still clenched at the thought that he had invited

another woman to their apartment on his lunch hour to take a pregnancy test. Luckily, she'd gotten home from work before him and found the evidence—along with pieces of the new mommy's lingerie when she'd gone through his side of the closet and thrown everything out of it. When Jeff had come in and sputtered that he bought those items as a surprise for her, she'd pointed out that a B-cup bra wouldn't cover *one* of her breasts, and after three years he should have known that.

"Here you go!" Paula made another hectic entrance into her office, handing off the flight information and thanking her profusely. "I have to run, my meeting's starting. Now, Evan's sweet but a bit of a smart ass. Don't let him give you any trouble. And just e-mail me the link to the web page when it's finished. You're a darling!"

Bree chugged the last of her diet soda and listened to Paula's stilettos click across the lobby on their way to the conference room. Considering the older woman's personality, it didn't surprise her that the younger Willett had a bit of spunk as well. Surely he couldn't irritate her too much during a twenty-minute drive.

According to the itinerary, she needed to get going in a couple of hours unless she wanted to leave Paula's kin stranded, which wouldn't make a great impression. She tossed her empty drink bottle into the waste can and tapped furiously on the keys.

Feeling Dirty? The Latest Innovation From Paula's Pleasure House Promises Hours Of Naughty, Clean Fun. Get Wet Today!

Damn.

Evan took a sip from his Styrofoam cup, vaguely aware of a burning sensation on his tongue. His whole body could have been on fire and he doubted he would notice. He'd fixed all his senses on a woman who stood near the ice cream freezer, staring out into the throngs of people who passed back and forth across the airport corridor.

Her hair was three different shades of brunette, a sleek bob that showed off graceful shoulders and a neck made for kissing. He couldn't see her face, but her backside provided a view so magnificent a man should have been charged by the minute just to look at it. He could easily imagine lowering the zipper that traced her spine and slipping off that deliciously tight dress...

Oh, yeah. If he didn't already have plans to visit Paula tonight, he'd put the moves on this woman. He needed a release, preferably the sexual kind. His head still throbbed from the shrieks of the child sitting behind him on the plane, a sound he had added to his long list of reasons for seeking permanent bachelorhood. Now he ached for some very grown-up attention.

A second sip of coffee nearly melted his lips. He cursed and jerked away from the cup, then put it on the table with a sigh. After two weeks away on business and almost no sleep, was a good caffeine fix so much to ask?

Thankfully, he had just one day left at this wretched consulting job. He'd spent half his life edging toward the top rung of the corporate ladder, and finally, just weeks away from his self-imposed deadline, Paula had offered him the perfect opportunity. But as usual, she was late picking him up, so he had a few more minutes to admire the delectable assets of the mystery woman.

At least, until she turned around and caught him watching her. His leisurely gaze morphed into a full-blown stare. She looked incredibly familiar. Where had he seen her before? Her features twisted in what appeared to be an effort to retrieve him from her memory as well.

She squinted, then took a step back. Her eyes widened and her jaw dropped to form a horrified "O". That face...

14

Barry's.

They had met at Barry's Lounge. A long time ago, probably several months back. It was her. It had to be. No one else had ever looked at him with an expression of such panic—and in the bedroom, no less. It hadn't exactly boosted his ego to sleep with a woman and have her answer his efforts with a covert escape. He'd never forget stepping out of the shower and finding her gone, then peering out the window in time to see her jump into her car and speed away. He'd been confused. Hurt. Pissed off.

And his long-awaited chance to chew her out had just arrived.

He abandoned the table and the coffee, raring to confront her. He was no stranger to one-night stands, but something about the way she'd scurried out when he wasn't looking ate at him to no end. Casual sex was one thing, but being used as an anonymous human vibrator pushed a line of disrespect he'd drawn after he had worked his way out of the slums.

He flashed her an innocent smile. "Get lost on your way to the bathroom?"

The way her eyes narrowed left no question that she knew what he meant. She folded her arms across her generous chest and examined his wrinkled clothes and unshaven face, the results of a day's worth of traveling. "A classy guy like you hasn't had anything else to think about for the past six months?"

"I'm sorry, was I supposed to dress up for you?"

"I wouldn't expect that from someone who pierces his face."

Several of the coffee shop's patrons craned their necks to see what she was talking about. Evan fumed, but he refused to defend his appearance to her or anyone else. The small ring in his brow held a significance they could never understand.

"I hate to tell you this," he said, "but if you wanted to intimidate me, you shouldn't have run away like a scared kid."

Her eyes matched the green of the ocean on a postcard he'd picked up before leaving Virginia. Abruptly, they shifted away from him.

"Back off." Her voice had lost much of its bite. "I'm expecting someone here and it sure isn't you."

"Oh, darn." He snapped his fingers, scanning the cafe for another familiar face.

Where on earth was she? He flew so much that Paula had generously offered to play chauffeur to save him outrageous parking fees. They always met in the same place, and he knew he'd faxed the itinerary to her. Flipping his mobile phone open, he pressed her speed dial button and smirked at the woman in front of him just for spite.

She glared at him and paced between the tables with her hands stuck on her hips. He didn't remember her being quite that gorgeous—or irate—the first time they'd met. But it had been dark and he'd downed a few drinks by that point.

"I've been waiting for half an hour," he greeted his sister when she answered. "What's the hold up, Paula?"

His acquaintance froze at the sound of the name.

"Didn't you get my voice mail? I'm busy at work and I sent one of my employees to pick you up. Isn't she there?"

Silence.

"Evan? Hello? Bree Jamison. She's tall, short hair, black—"

"Black dress...right. Never mind." His hand and the phone slipped from his ear and came to a stop on his shoulder. "I found her."

The din of the simultaneous conversations going on around him faded. That woman who had left so quickly yet stayed on his mind for months...the one who piqued his interest and his anatomy at the same time he wanted to put his hands around her slender, kissable neck for treating him like a fool. She was his ride.

She was Paula's employee.

Interesting.

He strode toward her until the gap between them had shrunk to no more than a couple of inches, and those sea-green eyes locked onto his in a heated power struggle. "You're a regular chameleon, aren't you? A sex kitten in the nightclub, then a timid schoolgirl in bed, now on the staff of one of the hottest fantasy sites in America. So, who are you, really?"

Bree's mouth opened. She pointed an accusing finger at him. "You're Paula's 'little brother'? *You?*"

"Looks like you better take back all those nasty things you just said to me."

"I respect Paula, not you."

"Obviously. If you had a scrap of respect for me, you would have stuck around long enough to find out my name."

"I wasn't interested in knowing it."

He snorted. "Really? That's not the impression I got when you threw yourself all over me at the bar."

"Don't flatter yourself. I was drunk and on the rebound, so let it go." She almost growled those last words.

Curiosity tugged at him. She looked upset about what had happened between them, but he couldn't muster the compassion to discuss it with her. When the vixen from the club had turned modest in his bedroom, he'd pegged her as a coddled rich girl out of her element. He had no soft emotions for the coddled or the rich.

He sighed. "You know what, this is ridiculous. I'll get a cab."

She grabbed his arm, dismantling his desire to give her a taste of her own rudeness and replacing it with a much more powerful need. A tingle generated on the patch of skin her fingers touched, and the sensation traveled through his arm before making its way down to his groin.

"No." She yanked her hand back like she'd put it in a flame. "I told Paula I'd get you to her place so you can pick up your car. I'll get you there. Just quit being so cocky and forget you ever knew me."

"Wouldn't that be nice," he said, but he was beginning to think otherwise.

They exited the airport, and he followed her to the parking garage. The inviting curves of her hips and ass swung back and forth with every step she took. Bree Jamison spelled luscious eye candy if nothing else.

He eyed her black sport sedan with appreciation, but he couldn't resist throwing out one more jab. "Not bad. Definitely not the minivan I expected from a prudish lass like yourself."

"Get in the car."

He obliged, biting back a grin. It had been a while since he'd done anything but work, and there wasn't room at his clients' conference tables for witty banter with beautiful women. But as much as Bree's spirited personality and foxy looks tempted him, he would have to find another outlet for his physical needs. She'd proven once that she wasn't the eager, sensual lover he had envisioned. That discovery continued to sorely disappoint him.

With a spark of hope that she'd somehow changed over the past few months, Evan watched her profile from the corner of his eye. Nope. Sex definitely remained the last thing on her mind. She kept her eyes fixed on the road, her fingers clenched around the wheel, apparently primed to drop him off as soon as possible and disregard his existence for the second time.

Oh, well. They would certainly run into each other in the days to come, but she didn't seem to know that and he didn't intend to tell her. If her past actions were any indication, her presence at the office would hardly be a challenge to his impending authority.

Bree's face still burned later that evening when she stalked into the gym and threw her duffel bag in the direction of two treadmills Jessica had claimed. It landed at her friend's feet with a resounding thump.

"You are dead. You are so dead."

Without breaking her pace, Jessica stuck out her arms. "What did I do?"

Bree turned her machine on, setting the speed higher than she normally did with the purpose of sweating off negative energy. "I picked up my boss's brother at the airport today."

"Yeah?"

"And it was the guy."

"What guy?"

"The guy from Barry's!" A woman lifting weights looked her way, and she lowered her voice. "*The guy.* The one you bet me I wouldn't have the nerve to pick up. Remember? 'Oh, Bree, one night with him will wipe Jeff from your mind.' And then I ended up sleeping with him and now I'll regret it for the rest of my life."

Jessica's face lit up. "The guy with the eyebrow ring?"

"Yes!"

"Sweet!"

"No!" Bree pounded her fist on the handrail, failing to understand how Jessica could not see the perils of her situation. "Not sweet, Jess. This is not sweet. He's my boss's *brother*. And he hates my guts. That can't be helpful to my career. What if he tells her?"

Jessica wiped moisture from her forehead. "What if he does? She probably doesn't want to think about her brother's sex life. God knows I don't want to."

"Your brother is twelve."

"And someday, heaven help us, he'll have a sex life."

"It's scary that you'd even think about that, Jess."

"Look, just because he's related to Paula doesn't mean you'll be seeing him. He doesn't work there, for crying out loud. You guys just had a run-in. You'll probably never see him again."

She hoped not. The more she thought about her random night with him, the less repulsive it seemed. The last thing she needed was a crush on someone who'd seen her at her most humiliating moment, yet she'd spent their brief car ride fighting the pull of attraction. She hadn't remembered him being so tall, or having that tousled bedroom hair and those chocolate-brown eyes set between long, dark lashes.

She hadn't noticed much about him at all during their first meeting, because she'd been too busy feeling like an idiot and wishing her way out of his bed. No wonder he'd been surprised to find out she worked for Paula. Her bashful response to their fooling around had been nowhere near worthy of the dildos and role-play costumes she spent her days presenting to the public.

She stared at the mirrored wall in front of her as the realization sunk in. Then she shut off her machine and watched her pace slow down and come to a complete stop. Kind of like her love life.

"Hey." Jessica stepped off the treadmill and gave her a concerned look. "Is something else bothering you?"

That was an understatement. Though she touted her job as the pinnacle of her "new" personality, she hadn't changed at all. Not only had she made excuses to avoid men since her disastrous night with Evan, but she'd been so rattled upon seeing him in the airport that she'd resorted to shallow insults, the kind of response she would expect from Jeff or her socialite parents.

She felt like hanging her head in shame. And how could she call herself anything but conservative when she hadn't touched a man in six months?

"I failed," she said.

Jessica gathered their bags and led Bree to a bench out of earshot of the few people left on the equipment. "At?"

"At broadening my horizons." She pulled a folded piece of paper from her purse and smoothed it over her leg. "This to-do list you made for me after Jeff and I broke up? I haven't touched it."

Jessica took the paper. "Sure you have. Number one, sex with a guy you don't love. Check."

"There are fourteen other things on the list!"

Jess eyed her. "And you haven't done any of them? Not even..." She scanned the page for an easy one. "Number six?"

"In your dreams." Or rather, in *her* dreams. That entire list amounted to nothing more than a tiny piece of Jessica's reality. Her friend had a foolproof ability to pick up men with huge sexual repertoires.

Jeff, on the other hand, wouldn't have put his mouth down where number six suggested in a million years. His moves had consisted solely of things that led to his own pleasure, and she'd been complacent enough to put up with it.

"You can't be serious." Jessica glanced at the list again. "No sixty-nine? No sex in a public place?"

Bree shook her head.

"Girl, you're missing out."

"No kidding. I feel like a mutant. I'm twenty-six and I've never had hot, sweaty, to-die-for sex."

Jess laughed and patted her hand. "That can be remedied, you know. I know you want the white wedding and six kids and all that—"

"But I'm not getting married any time soon," Bree finished for her, an idea forming. She was light years from finding Mr. Right, but when he did come around, she didn't want to blow it the way she had with Evan. *Practice makes perfect...*

Jessica grinned. "Right. So it sounds to me like you didn't *fail* to complete the list, you just experienced a delay."

"I like the way you think."

"Trust me, sweetie. It's like I told you after the breakup. You get to the end of that list, you'll be a new woman."

Bree smiled. A new woman. One who could back up her sensual web pages with experience rather than imagination and Internet research. She'd wasted a lot of years waiting for a ring instead of enjoying the pleasures of skilled, naked men without worrying about what—or who—they did when she wasn't around. No harm in making up that time now and securing a fabulous career in the process.

Chapter Two

On Thursday morning, Bree perched on the edge of her seat in the conference room, waiting to hear what her boss had up her lace-covered sleeve. Rumor had it today's staff meeting would involve more than the usual updates and assignments, and if Paula wanted to drop a huge project on her, Bree was ready.

She needed something to drag her mind away from Monday's unexpected reunion with Evan. After a few days of expecting to see him around every corner, she had accepted that Jessica was right. Their encounter at the airport had been a one-time deal and she wouldn't see him again.

Nothing would please her more. To complete the list and gain enough sexual expertise to cinch the career and the man of her dreams, she needed to think like a siren who could please any man, not face the living, breathing reminder that she hadn't even opened her eyes the last time she'd been in a guy's bed.

Beside her, Todd pulled out a chair and whipped it around, straddling it backward. "I think this is it."

"It?"

"The moment you've been waiting for. The day Paula hires you on for good."

Bree's eyes widened, her heart twirling at the possibility.

"But I've still got a few weeks left in my contract."

He shrugged. "Doesn't matter. You've done incredible work, and there's no rule that says she can't make her decision before your last day."

"True, there isn't." She smiled. If she received a full-time offer today, she could build her collection of steamy experiences faster since she wouldn't be working so many hours trying to prove Paula needed her.

"Anyway, I'd sure like to see you stay with us," Todd continued. "You're the only other person who knows the way around the website, and if you'll excuse my selfishness, I'd like to spend more time with my family."

His sheepish expression made her laugh. This office wasn't a place where a man had to apologize for making his family a priority. "I doubt anyone would blame you for that. Sasha and the boys are great."

He looked down at the gold band encircling his finger. "Well, it's baseball season, and we've been so busy here. I don't want to miss a game."

"I promise, if Paula hires me, I'll make sure you don't." Considering she didn't have anyone waiting for her at home, the least she could do was free up someone who did. Todd's eight-year-old twins were baseball fanatics, and he had attended every practice and game since their T-ball days.

"Big news, everybody!"

In typical fashion, Paula's voice arrived before her body. She breezed in and clasped her hands in front of the oversized whiteboard, beaming at her thirteen employees.

Bree held her breath, hoping to hear Todd's prediction come true. Talking about his kids reminded her how far she had to go before a gold band or pregnancy test would belong to her. She ached to stop worrying about her job security and start ticking items off the list, which was currently burning a hole in her purse.

"Business is booming," Paula began, "and I know a lot of you are overworked. To lighten some of the load with summer vacations starting up, I've decided we could use another hand to help out our sales and marketing efforts."

The room filled with inquisitive murmurs. Bree looked gleefully at Todd, who gave her a thumbs-up. The thought of being a permanent fixture at PPH overjoyed her. No more bending to outdated social standards, no more sleeping alone every night. Armed with a sizzling career and an even hotter record of sexual escapades, she'd blow her old identity—the girl who'd been lied to, cheated on, and abandoned—right off the map.

"So." Paula reached for the conference room door, her hand pausing on the knob. "I've hired a marketing consultant. He'll start by analyzing our site, determining if we're reaching our customers as effectively as we can, and helping out with design and content."

Bree's enthusiasm tapered. A marketing consultant?

That was definitely *not* a job offer, and it didn't sound like a rookie who'd be a step below her, either. In fact, it sounded a lot like someone who would constantly look over her shoulder and question her efforts. She'd be answering to an additional boss when she thrived on being left to her own imagination.

The first pangs of dread churned in her stomach.

"Rest assured our relationship will not affect my evaluation of his work. This is a small company, and you're all like family to me. It's fitting, then, that today I'd like to introduce a highly successful consultant and also my brother, Evan Willett."

No.

No!

She couldn't look. The room spun. Her digestive system revolted. Her colleagues applauded and exchanged hellos with the newcomer, but she just kept her head down and tried to burn a hole in her notepad with her eyes.

Evan, a marketing consultant? Impossible. She'd pictured him as a blue-collar type of guy, or a dropout from one of the local universities. He was what, maybe twenty-two or twenty-three? Not old enough to be giving her orders, she knew that much.

Finally, slowly, curiosity won over and she dared to glance up at the man standing in front of the group.

Oh, was she in trouble.

She wouldn't have recognized him if not for his ever-present brow ornament. Gone were the crumpled jeans and T-shirt he had worn in the coffee shop, having been replaced by beige dress pants and a navy blue polo shirt. His face was clean-shaven and not one strand of his hair, a deep shade of brown that looked black from a distance, fell out of place.

He looked ten years older than she had guessed.

He was gorgeous.

"Thanks, everyone." With a big grin, Evan hooked his thumbs into his belt loops and rocked back on his heels. "I'm thrilled to have the opportunity to work with all of you, and with a product line I'd like to think I'm an expert on."

The staff laughed. At least, most of them did. Bree scowled, torn between her loathing of his arrogance and her sudden urge to find out how much he knew about the many uses of their sensual products.

"I'll be spending most of my time with the graphic design team," he said. "Who's in charge of that?"

She hoped no one would draw attention to her even as heads began to turn in her direction. Todd created the graphics and transferred them to her, and she put them together with her written content to produce pages that generated public interest and customer orders. The two of them *were* the graphic and web design team, as well as the marketing department. They handled everything seen by the public eye—everything Evan appeared ready to discuss.

Why was this happening to her?

Todd gave her a nod, as did Paula. She should have been ecstatic at being acknowledged as the person in charge, but she couldn't calm the queasiness that sloshed through her at the prospect of having to deal with Evan every single day.

Gathering her courage, she offered him a smile void of warmth and rose from her chair. "That would be me."

His forehead wrinkled in surprise, and the contempt they shared for each other crept into his eyes. "You? It's Bree, right?"

She smirked at his juvenile charade. She could only wish they'd just met.

"Hmm. I pictured you more as an accounting type of girl."

That did it. His references to her girlhood and boring nature were wearing on her nerves. Not to mention he seemed to have no idea that the company's accountant was a sassy redhead known for owning Paula's complete line of S&M attire.

She couldn't let him base his opinion of her on those brainless minutes she'd spent in his bed. Her shy and conservative days were over; she had made that decision at the gym. She'd adhered to the rules and expectations of her family's uppity, overly-traditional social circle for years because she thought it would be worth it when she earned a lifelong marriage, two-point-five kids and a dog, just like everyone else she knew. Her cousin. Her neighbor. The girls from her old prep school. They were all building futures with men who'd courted them since adolescence.

Not Bree. Her years of being a faithful and loving girlfriend had left her with nothing but a broken heart and a trashed self-image, at least until she'd started working at Paula's Pleasure House. No one here knew or cared about her upbringing, so she could be whatever person she wanted to be. She loved the daily opportunities to explore the kind of fun she'd only seen in the pay-per-view flicks Jessica had watched in college.

Evan threatened to ruin every bit of it. Comments like the one he'd just made would wreak havoc on her sexy new image. She couldn't have her coworkers—especially Paula—questioning whether a proper girl like her belonged at a footloose place like PPH.

Nice girls finished last. She'd learned that the hard way. And though she couldn't get started on the list in the middle of the office, she could grab the reins of the one adventure she already had going for her—her career. At least for the next three weeks.

"Sorry to disappoint you, but I'm the senior web designer. I write all of the content you find on the site, and any changes you're interested in making will be discussed with me before they go into effect."

There. She crossed her arms and met his astonished gaze, confident in her ability to stand her ground and defend her job even with someone as infuriating and sexy as Evan threatening to take over.

"The content. The product descriptions, the tips and tricks—you write all of that?"

"Every word."

He nodded slowly, his scornful expression fading. "Impressive."

"Thank you. I'm quite competent at what I do, Mr. Willett." She gave herself a mental kick for flirting, and she hoped her coworkers wouldn't notice the double meaning in her statement.

Judging from the pause that ensued, he got the point. "Call me Evan."

She could think of plenty of names she'd like to call him.

Jackass and *love slave* came to mind first, though she wasn't sure in what order.

He chatted with a few of the other employees before the meeting adjourned. Bree hightailed back to her office, closing her door so she could have a moment alone to figure out what in the world she was going to do. Each of her closest friends, Jessica, Lynn and Tara-Beth, had managed to end up involved with a coworker at some point or another, and Evan was a disaster that warranted their advice.

She typed the world's fastest email requesting that her pals meet her for dinner and zipped it off to all three of them. The moment she hit "Send" a knock sounded on the door.

"Come in."

Paula stuck her head inside. "Hey. Sorry to bother you so soon, but I was wondering if you'd have a chance to show Evan some of the ropes today. You know, the web software, some of the standard procedural stuff..."

"Of course. What time is he available?" *Anything for this job*, Bree reminded herself, even while she fought the persistent urge to throw up.

The door opened wider and Evan appeared, his too-handsome face jubilant that his new career put him in such an ideal position to torment her.

"How about now?" His tone was more syrupy than a character on a children's television show.

Paula raised her eyebrows expectantly.

Bree forced the right answer out of her mouth. "Sure. Come on in."

Evan thanked his sister and shut the door behind him. Great. They were alone in an enclosed space, not even a single window available for escape.

"So." He sat in a nearby chair, plopped his shoes on top of

her desk and crossed his feet. He was purposely trying to aggravate her, and damn if he didn't do it well. "Enlighten me with your knowledge, Bree Jamison."

If they had been anywhere else, she'd have broken a few of his toes with her heavy-duty stapler. But attacking Evan wouldn't score any points with his sister, so she pointed a sharp letter opener at him instead. "Take your legs off my desk. Now."

"What? I couldn't hear you."

She threw the opener in a drawer and slammed it shut, getting to her feet. "Fine. If I don't teach you this stuff, you'll have nothing to *consult*, big shot. But since you're so smart, you can learn it yourself."

When she made a move to leave, he dropped his legs and jumped out of the chair. He seized her hand. "Bree, wait. I want to talk."

There it was again. The glare that told Evan she would kill him if given the chance. Of course, she had threatened him with that letter opener...

Her hand. He was still holding her hand. Flustered, he dropped it and turned away from the enticing bit of cleavage peering out from the top of her blouse before the need to taste her skin consumed him.

Bree crossed her arms. "What could you possibly want to talk about?"

"I want to talk about the possibility of us trying to get along, since we'll be working together quite a bit."

Her forehead crinkled with indifference. "Whatever."

He sighed. The chip on her shoulder seemed to have his name engraved on it, and that could spell trouble for his upcoming promotion. He hadn't expected the tamest lover of his life to grow a temper the moment he walked into the office.

"I don't get you. What is your deal? Is this that much of a problem for you?" He pointed to his eyebrow ring, which she had made a point to criticize in the airport along with the rest of his appearance. It was a wonder she'd gone home with him in the first place if she believed he was such a rogue.

She pulled open a file drawer and sifted through its contents. "It's really not my style."

"It doesn't have to be your style. I also have a tattoo, wanna see?"

The drawer slammed shut. "No!"

"I don't see how you work here. You're so damned conservative."

She glanced down at her miniskirt and the boots that reached halfway up her thighs, absurdly thinking he meant her appearance rather than her personality. He was about to correct her when she unbuttoned the top of her blouse, leaned forward, and showed him what she wore underneath it.

"Is that too conservative for you?" she asked.

He swallowed, taking in the spectacular sight of the red bustier that clung to Bree's waist and shaped her breasts into perfect spheres of flesh he ached to touch. Maybe he'd been a little quick to judge her as the shy type. He cleared his throat and held his clipboard in front of his pants in a pathetic attempt to hide his arousal.

"Um. Red is...definitely your color. But I'm not sure you should be sashaying around the workplace in your lingerie."

"You don't seem to mind." With a glance at his clipboard, she closed her blouse and then returned to her desk. "If we're going to get along, you need to drop this whole nice-girl impression you have."

"It's the only impression you've given me."

"You don't know me at all."

Maybe not, but he wanted to. Her new attitude reminded him of the woman he'd been so attracted to at the club, the bold, sexy lover he had imagined her to be until she'd virtually shut down in his bedroom. The lost possibilities of that night played in his mind like a recurring dream. Was it possible to redo a one-night stand?

He moved toward her, skimming her body with his gaze even though his hands itched to do the work. She must have sensed the way he mentally undressed her, because a shaky breath moved through her parted lips and she backed into her desk. He imagined shoving everything off and making love to her right on top of it, just like a scene from a cheesy movie. It didn't seem so cheesy when he was growing hotter by the second and the focus of his desire stood right in front of him, close enough to taste.

"I tried to spend more time with you that night," he said. "If you'll recall, I asked you to join me in the shower. Instead of taking me up on a second—and third and fourth—round, you took the opportunity to leave."

Bree's eyes widened when he said *third*, and they nearly bulged at the word *fourth*.

Yeah, she was a nice girl, even if she wouldn't admit it. And he'd relive his worst day in poverty to find out how she'd ended up writing erotic promotional text for a kinky toy store.

On second thought...maybe not his *worst* day. He touched his brow ring in a tribute to the man who lived on in his memory. The day he'd lost his best friend was forever etched in his mind regardless of Bree's career choice. But he sure wanted to know what had caused her personality transplant.

"Don't bring that up ever again, and we might have a chance at getting along." She sat in her chair, avoiding his eyes. The animosity had drained from her voice. She clutched her mouse and searched for a program on her computer. "Just sit down and I'll take you through this stuff."

For the second time that week, Evan wondered what it was about having slept with him that made her so uncomfortable. A disturbing thought jigged in the back of his mind, but he ignored it. She couldn't have been a virgin when they'd met. She'd been too sexy, too sure of herself in the club. And she hadn't hesitated when they had burst into his apartment, ripping each other's clothes off.

So why had she frozen up once they were naked, and why had she run away when it was over?

He itched to know the story behind that drama, but Bree had finished discussing it. At least he'd accomplished something—they were speaking civilly. Sort of. He tried his best to pay attention as she guided him through the ins and outs of the website, but banner ads for leopard-print thongs, flavored body paints and various other goodies flooded his brain with visions of the ways they could try out those items together.

And when he saw the pink on her cheeks and how fast she clicked around to find a page free of intimate pictures, he ached to make her blush with need, not embarrassment.

He willed himself to concentrate. He couldn't very well run the company if something as simple as an attractive woman distracted him. Now wasn't the time for screwing around, literally or figuratively. Paula needed a successor, and they had always been each other's greatest support system during hard times. His sister was coming up on some formidable times, and he'd promised to be on his best behavior.

He'd also promised Tony on the night of the accident that within ten years, he would carry out their shared dream— working for themselves instead of The Man. Eating from a silver spoon instead of scaring the local burger joint cashier into handing over a couple of sandwiches. That anniversary was coming up next month, around the same time Paula would decide whether to make him CEO. One mistake and he'd let down the two people he loved most.

When he thought of it that way, hooking up with his coworker would have to wait.

When Bree had asked her friends for help regarding her situation with Evan, she'd been looking for advice on how to work with him while ignoring their past. She'd forgotten that the girls were strongly against ignoring sex. In fact, she suspected they were on a mission to do it as many times as possible in as many *ways* as possible, all before the age of thirty.

Tara-Beth swiped her piece of bread through a plate of olive oil. "Well, I had a problem with that tech support guy I dated when I worked the graveyard shift. He forgot to disconnect his last caller before we got busy on his desk. Guess we were a little too loud, because the customer complained and we both got fired."

Jessica and Lynn giggled. Bree shook her head.

"The thing is," Lynn added, "you have to make sure you hide your relationship while you're actually in the office. After hours, he's all yours."

Bree made a grunting noise and unfolded her napkin so harshly she sent a spoon careening to the floor. A passing waitress quickly offered to bring another.

"You guys are missing the point. Evan and I aren't dating. We slept together that one awful night, and now I have to look at him, and talk to him... I have to discuss the proper way to market dildos with him! Every single day! How am I supposed to deal with that without dying of embarrassment?"

"It was just sex," Jessica replied, poking her salad with a fork. "You're acting like it's the end of the world."

A headache formed behind Bree's eyes. She dug a couple of aspirin from her purse and downed them with a glass of water. Her friends were great—smart, funny, always there when she needed them—but all three had a knack for casual dating she had never picked up. They were so different from her. Their friendship wouldn't even exist if they hadn't shared a suite during their first year at UCLA. In retrospect, it had been the best thing that could have happened to her. Jess, Lynn and Tara-Beth had been the first people in her life who hadn't demanded she fit into her family's uptight mold.

But as much as she envied their easygoing nature, their affinity for short-term affairs had never rubbed off on her. As far as she was concerned, relationships were all or nothing. She never went out with a man unless she already knew him well enough to know she'd be comfortable around him and the relationship would have a chance at lasting. The idea of kissing a guy who wouldn't remember her name the next day had a fun factor right up there with food poisoning.

Knowing that, she'd still gone and slept with Evan Willett, Total Stranger. Stranger with a piece of metal in his face—and a tattoo! The only piercings one would have found in her private high school were on the girls—and only in their ears, if they wanted to avoid social alienation. Where she came from, people associated that kind of stuff with trouble, kids from the "wrong side of the tracks".

Not that she gave a lot of credit to such meaningless labels. Jeff had been a medical student from a prominent family, and look how well *that* had turned out.

But for crying out loud, Evan wasn't an ex-boyfriend who'd come back to haunt her. That would have been merely awkward—this was mortifying. He had witnessed the paralyzing moment she'd been slammed with regret over her decision to ignore her values and sleep with a stranger—right in the middle of the action, no less. He had seen her naked and exposed as less proficient in the sack than most sixteen-year-olds. And now he oversaw her projects at work, projects that were blatantly, unavoidably sexual. Was she being punished for taking her friends up on a stupid dare?

"I knew I shouldn't have agreed to that bet," she mumbled.

Jessica heard her. "Hey, don't you remember how much fun we had that night?"

"At Barry's? Yeah, it was great. For a while."

"Bree, you loved it," Lynn pointed out. "I've never seen you so uninhibited. Singlehood looked fabulous on you."

"And you see where it got me."

"It got you to bed with a *fine* piece of man." Jessica paused to chew a crouton. "Come on, think about it. Was it really that bad?"

Yes, she wanted to shout. The three of them had taken her to Barry's for a girl's night out, because nearly eight weeks after she'd kicked Jeff to the curb, she was still wallowing in depression and hadn't left her place for anything but work and groceries. Ignoring her objections, they'd gussied her up and taken her man-hunting.

Right away, she'd spotted Evan leaning on the bar. His dark clothes and brooding disposition were not at all her type, but the masculinity and hint of danger surrounding him attracted her in a purely physical way. She always fantasized about such men despite knowing full well that she would never want to date one. Unfortunately, she'd made the mistake of revealing that information to her best friends.

They had razzed her about it all night, taking turns approaching him to find out his marital status and other important tidbits—boxers or briefs?—while Bree sat at their table nursing a drink, first humiliated, then amused, and eventually convinced that getting over Jeff would require doing something completely off the wall and that might be her chance.

But she'd hesitated, until her friends bet her that she didn't have the nerve to ask him to leave with her. And if she did? All three of them would go to the ladies' room, strip down to nothing but the G-strings beneath their tight dresses, and saunter back through the crowded club and out the front door.

She couldn't pass up the chance to return the mortification they'd brought upon her by dragging her downtown for an evening at a virtual meat market. So, laying the flattery and innuendo on thick, she had picked up Evan. In a bit of a daiquiri-and-adrenaline-induced daze, she had so much fun flirting that she'd forgotten about the bet—until she glanced in her rearview mirror on her way to his place and spotted her friends jumping around topless outside the club, whooping and waving at her as they struggled to pull their clothes back on and get to their cars before the police showed up.

She started laughing and couldn't stop. The waiter brought their plates, and her eyes were watering by the time he left. "I can't believe you guys did that!"

Tara-Beth grinned. "That's not what you were supposed to be thinking about."

"Okay, fine. It wasn't that bad. I guess." She took a bite of her steaming pasta, then yelped and reached for her water. Waving her hand in front of her mouth, she continued, "I mean, he did have the hottest body I've ever seen."

Jessica nodded in approval. "That's a start."

"Was he...?" Lynn twirled her long brown curls, her eyes motioning downward. "You know—blessed? In the man department?"

Bree didn't want to think about her knowledge of Evan's man department when she would be sitting next to him again in a matter of hours. "I don't remember, guys. It was over before I could really tell."

Actually, she did remember. Quite well. If the signature of a blessed man included a sore bottom the next day, then she could answer Lynn's question with an emphatic yes. She'd been with Evan long enough to recognize that he had the potential to really please a woman—if he were paying attention.

But he hadn't paid attention to her. He'd consumed her body like a wild animal, which might not have been so bad if she'd joined the party instead of focusing her energy on her rumpled pile of clothes in an attempt to beam them back on. She'd been as active as a rag doll lying there, and that hadn't helped anything. The whole episode was a huge mistake she had initiated, but still, she loathed the way he'd poked at her like he'd bought her off the clearance page at PPH. Maybe she wouldn't regret it so much if he had shown some concern for her feelings. How would it feel if he truly made love to her? The startling question almost caused her to choke on her next bite.

Briefly, she wished she hadn't laid eyes on him until this morning's meeting. He'd be a good candidate for helping her strike several items off the list if he didn't already think she sucked in bed.

She mulled that over while she finished her dinner. He was evaluating her job performance, and though she always turned in quality work, she wouldn't put it past him to let his disdain for her color his judgment. Not to mention she was sick of being a virtual nun—that was the reason she had taken the unconventional job in the first place.

If Evan believed she was a sexual dud, there were strong incentives for changing his mind.

Chapter Three

"This whole site seems to assume that everyone looking at it knows exactly what they want. Maybe we should designate separate areas for men and women, or pages that are easier to navigate for customers who need suggestions. I mean, if I'd never seen a vibrator before, I would be lost here."

Bree chewed her bottom lip, trying not to laugh at the somber tone of Evan's voice. He sounded like he was discussing world events instead of sex toys.

"So, you've had a lot of experience with those," she said.

"With what?"

"Vibrators."

He turned his hypnotic brown irises on her. "I've seen a few."

She gave him I-told-you-so eyes, pressing her bottom against her chair to quell the tingling sensation that surfaced when she placed Evan and a vibrator in the same mental image. Thankfully, it was almost the weekend. Her hormones needed a couple of days to recover from his maddeningly erotic presence.

"Let me guess. My vibrator awareness has confirmed your belief that I'm a raging Casanova."

"Pretty much."

"Fine. Then the fact that you've never seen one confirms my belief that you're a frigid goody-two-shoes."

She felt her cheeks flush a shade that matched her clothing. She'd taken extra time getting ready that morning and put on her favorite red halter dress, the one that showed off the results of her long hours on the treadmill. But Evan still couldn't see past her modest response to their affair.

She hated that term, *goody-two-shoes.* Admittedly, her character hadn't caught up with her risqué clothing yet, but she had every intention of changing that. In fact, she was close to conquering number four on the list—buying a sex toy.

And having Evan show her how to use it.

"What makes you think I've never seen one?" she demanded.

He raised that silver ring at her, his eyes ablaze. "You're practically drooling on the screen. Curiosity getting the best of you?"

Curiosity was nearly killing her. Her eyes were open to the thrill of hot sex now, and somehow, she knew that a second time with him would erase every memory of their first meeting.

But she couldn't take the honest approach, not yet. They were barely treading friendly waters, and she couldn't lose the upper hand until she'd convinced him that his original impression of her had been way off-base.

"I can see I'll have to prove you wrong." Her fingers wrapped around the handle of her bottom drawer and pulled it out so hard the entire desk rattled. Inside lay a hefty collection of vibrators in different colors, textures, and sizes.

Evan looked down at the array of fake penises and threw his head back in amusement. Chuckling, he managed to say, "I'm afraid work-related devices don't count."

"You didn't say that. You said I'd never seen one."

"I amend my earlier statement. So you've seen one. But you've never *used* one."

He drew that word out like a long, slow lick on an ice cream cone. Bree-flavored ice cream. From behind those sultry eyelashes he watched her, daring her to be turned on by his proposition.

She wasn't merely turned on. She was a hungry lioness circling her cage, waiting for the door to open so she could burst out and devour a succulent piece of meat.

Yum.

She glanced at her office door to make sure it was closed. Time to put her seduction plan into action.

Swallowing hard, she reached into the drawer and retrieved a sizable blue cylinder. Her hand shook with nerves, so she squeezed her fingers around the thing more tightly. If she were going to refute his assumptions, she couldn't be afraid of a vibrator. She needed to act like she'd used one every day of her adult life. Like having a man watch her touch herself with one came as naturally as breathing.

A smile played on her lips. Letting a man watch *and* using a sex toy? She could knock two things off the list with this one simple act.

Simple. Right.

Her smile fading, she blew out a shaky breath and brushed the tip over her exposed shoulder, seeing Evan's mouth open just enough to let her know she had his interest. With excruciating slowness, she dragged the toy down her arm, making a U-turn at her wrist before bringing it back up and across her collarbone. She shivered at the cool, tingly trail it left on her skin and closed her eyes, wondering how she'd follow through with this show when she'd never even done it privately.

Before she got that far, Evan rolled his chair closer. Her eyes snapped open. His penetrating gaze fixed on her, he removed the device from her skin and held it tantalizingly in front of her face.

"What are you doing?" she objected.

He didn't answer, just turned it on with a single flick of his thumb. The purr of the tiny motor made her jump.

The way he stared at her made her feel naked even though she remained fully clothed. The room was nearly silent, the buzz of the fluorescent lights drowned out by the beat of her racing heart. She should have bashed his hand, should have bolted from the chair.

But she didn't.

"Don't touch me with that," she rasped. "Don't you dare."

Yet still she couldn't move. What was wrong with her? Evan's attempt to take control of the situation wasn't surprising, given his sky-high confidence level. But *enjoying* his power trip was not part of the plan.

"So." His breath caressed her neck as he dipped the pulsating tip into the top of her dress, grazing the cleft between her breasts. "Would you like a demonstration of what this thing is really used for?"

He looked down, and she knew he'd spotted her rigid nipples poking through the thin fabric of her outfit. Lovely. As cavalier as he was to begin with, she didn't want to reveal that, at the moment, her attraction to him was fueling her quest for sexual experience. Much as she hated to admit that, it was entirely, irrevocably true.

Her mind begged her to move away from him. *Your terms, remember?* But her body refused to listen. One more moment of his dizzying nearness, one more second of his warm breath grazing her skin just the way it had when he'd been inside her, and she would lose this battle. She'd be taking lessons from him instead of showing him what she could do.

So why did it feel so good?

An inkling of smugness in his smile, he moved the device down to her knee and began sliding it up the inside of her thigh. "I'll take that as a yes."

No, no, no!

"Evan—"

"Happy birthday!" The door flew open and the entire staff burst in, cake in tow. Snapping to attention, Bree watched in horror as the vibrator dropped from Evan's fingers and rolled underneath her desk. For once, he looked stunned as well. Thank God it was one of the quietest designs.

Her computer monitor hid their frolicking from view just long enough for them to compose themselves. Evan ran a hand through his dark hair, doing his best to appear casual. "Wow, you guys didn't have to do this."

Paula stepped up and hugged him. "Well, it's Friday afternoon and we could all use a break. Didn't want to ignore your big three-one." She turned to Bree. "Sorry I didn't warn you, but you two have been locked in here all day working on the site. I didn't want to interrupt and make anything look suspicious."

Bree smiled weakly. "No problem." If Paula only knew that *she* should have been the suspicious one.

They moved the party to the conference room, and Bree excused herself. The throbbing between her legs made it difficult to play social butterfly. She practically ran to the restroom. When she got there, she washed her hands under cold water and dabbed at her moist forehead with a paper towel.

What the hell was that? She glowered into the mirror. The idea was to prove she could be an assertive, sensual woman, not a submissive girl who'd let him do whatever he felt like doing to her. He already believed that, and she had just wiped away any progress they might have made on the path to understanding each other beyond their one-night stand.

Now she'd have to start over. You hate him, she insisted to

Avery Beck

her reflection. *You hate him.*

She didn't hate him. She knew it the moment she returned to the celebration and felt a twinge of jealousy in her gut when she saw him talking with Michelle, Paula's executive assistant. Short and thin, with straight black hair down to the small of her back, Michelle was barely old enough to drink and definitely too young for a veteran Romeo like Evan.

Judging from the way he smiled at the girl, Evan didn't designate a minimum age to his bedfellows. That, combined with the sight of Michelle wiping a bit of icing from his lips and obscenely licking it off her finger, reminded Bree that he'd pounce on anything with legs, and he had played her like a piano with the vibrator stint.

"Can you imagine—our esteemed marketing consultant having an affair with the secretary?" Lacy, the kinky accountant, approached in a fit of giggles, her fire-engine colored hair tied back in a bouncing ponytail.

Bree made a face as they watched the philandering take place across the room. "I don't know. She's a little young for him."

"Uh-uh. They have a date this weekend." Lacy held up her paper plate and half-eaten slice of chocolate cake. "Want some?"

Bree's chest tightened as a wave of senseless nausea hit. Evan was going on a date? Of all the people in the world or even the office, why would he pick Michelle?

Why did she care?

"No, thanks. I don't feel too well. Did he ask her out?"

"She asked him. They're going dancing or something, but she told me she'll end up at his place if it kills her." More giggling.

As the office Gossip Queen, Lacy had a vivid imagination and Bree wondered if—and hoped—she was exaggerating. When

44

she thought of Evan and Michelle getting hot and heavy in the same bed *she* and Evan had, she wanted to cram his birthday cake up his womanizing behind. Was she hallucinating, or had his hand been between her knees ten minutes ago?

Forget it. A glance at the wall clock revealed that her Evan-free weekend started in five minutes. She went back to her office to grab her purse, and the bleat of her cell phone announced a call from Jessica.

"Hey, Jess."

"Girl, you heading home?"

"Walking out the door right now."

"Good. Lynn got that promotion and we're going to Barry's tonight to celebrate. Want to bring Evan?"

She rolled her eyes at her friend's teasing, though a tiny, defiant part of her wished that were a possibility. "Ha, ha. You'll be lucky if I go at all."

"Oh, you'll go. You know we promised to pitch in and show her a good time when she made nurse practitioner."

"Don't get your panties in a bunch," she replied, using one of Jessica's favorite sayings against her. "I'll be there."

She clapped the phone shut and rooted around in her purse for her car keys. Barry's had been their primary hangout for years, but after her night of stupidity six months ago, she had pegged it The Place She Lost Her Mind. She only showed her face there when she had to, like she would in a few hours. Lynn's dream of being an obstetrical nurse had just come true, and her hard-earned achievement took precedence over Bree's frivolous dating problems.

The last few staff members trickled out of the conference room as she stepped into the hallway and locked her office door. She turned her back to avoid any sudden glimpses of Evan and Michelle drooling on each other, possibly feeding each other cake and then sharing a gooey, sugary kiss. Revolting.

Okay, forget Lacy—*her* imagination had spun out of control and her behavior matched that of an envious adolescent girl.

"Do you let all men fondle you before you abandon them, or is it just me?"

She'd recognize that deep voice and smart mouth anywhere.

Evan's hand rested on her shoulder and his fingers warmed her skin yet sent chills down to her toes. She'd never wear a halter dress to work again. Too many bare spots for him to touch.

"Man. Not one word at my own birthday party. I should be insulted."

Her key still stuck in the doorknob, she answered coolly, "Looked like you had your hands full. I didn't want to interrupt."

A slow snicker drifted into her ear. He leaned down and whispered, "You're jealous."

She jerked the key from the lock and turned to face him. "Of what? Five minutes of apathetic screwing? I sure don't want to miss one second of that."

She regretted the words the instant they left her mouth. Too harsh. Too much. His mammoth ego had finally destroyed her tact.

Hurt flickered in his cocoa eyes, but he didn't say anything. He just trapped her against the door between his muscular arms.

She tried not to look at them, instead squaring her shoulders in a weak attempt to hide her growing desire. "I have to go."

He didn't budge, nor did he take his eyes away from hers.

"Please move," she implored. "I think we're finished here."

A devilish grin spread across his face. "You think wrong.

We've only just begun."

Noting the heavy laptop case hanging over Bree's shoulder, the purse and keys she clutched in one hand, and a cardboard box that rested on her other elbow, Evan dropped his menacing pose and offered his hand. "Do you need some help?"

Her back still against the door, she fixed him with a disparaging gaze. "Let's get one thing straight. I'm not a damsel in distress, and you're no knight. I can manage."

A spitfire, she was. He took the box anyway, feeling oddly like he owed her something.

Five minutes of apathetic screwing. Was she serious?

Images of that evening at Barry's flashed through his head. Her dress, so low-cut it had almost exposed her navel. Her smile, promising a night of passion he'd never forget...and her eyes, dark and filled with the same emotion. He'd been so hot for her, he had talked consulting jargon to himself all the way back to his place just to keep from coming in the car.

When they'd finally reached the bed, he had expected a long, hot romp, one that explored half the positions of the Kama Sutra and ended with a friendly goodbye that acknowledged the need they'd fulfilled for each other. But Bree had been in such a hurry—at least, he thought she had. She'd closed her eyes and rejected his attempts to look at her, to feel her, to taste her.

He should have talked to her, maybe taken the time to make her feel comfortable if she thought they were moving too fast. But he never mixed emotion and sex, a dangerous combination that, as far as he could tell, led only to hardship and loss. So he'd given her the quickie he'd believed she wanted. Like he had told her at the office, he'd planned to make it up to her for the rest of the night if she changed her mind.

Unfortunately, she'd had plans to bolt. And his initial laziness hadn't gone unnoticed by the woman he had once concluded wouldn't know the difference between good sex and bad.

Now, he was sure she knew. And he could hardly contain his desire to demonstrate his usual skills and find out if she had hidden her proficiency as well.

He cleared his throat. "Let me walk you to your car."

Bree made a show of looking annoyed but allowed him to escort her through the building. He opened his mouth to ask her what she had in the box, then noticed that the label on it read none other than Paula's Pleasure House.

"Whoa!" he cried as they stepped into the elevator. "What's this? Do you take this stuff home and play with it?"

A rousing vision of her long, sleek body draped over a bed or sprawled on the floor practicing the same thing he'd tried to do to her earlier filled his mind, making him hard and aching to touch her again.

She looked to the ceiling as though begging for mercy. "It's for my friend."

"Really." Not believing that old line for a second, he put the box to his ear and shook it. "What is it? Too heavy to be the sort of thing we were playing with today."

"You know, I'd prefer if you never mentioned that again."

He almost spouted off another comment about jealousy, but her pained expression silenced him.

The elevator doors opened. They made their way into the parking area, and despite his better judgment, he asked, "What were you rebounding from?"

She walked slightly in front of him, and every muscle in her back tensed. Headlights flashed as she unlocked her car. "I don't know what you're talking about."

"You said you were drunk and on the rebound."

She threw her bags into the backseat, then took the box

from him and tossed it inside the trunk. "How many times do I have to tell you I don't want to talk about that?"

"What if I do?"

"It's complicated."

"Try me."

Sunlight glinted on the highlights in her hair, giving her a glow that didn't quite match the frown on her pretty face. She chewed her lower lip and squinted into the cloudless May sky before meeting his eyes again.

"My ex-boyfriend is expecting a baby any day now, if that tells you anything. And obviously it's not mine."

She ran her hands over her abdomen and he had to agree, it wasn't nine months pregnant. But it was beautiful. And sexy. And arousing—not at all an appropriate response to her situation.

"I'm sorry to hear that."

Her shoulders lifted. "Yeah, well, it's not like the first thing I wanted to do was jump into bed with another guy. My friends were trying to cheer me up and we made a stupid bet."

"A bet?" He vaguely recalled a few girls who had appeared next to him, asked him random questions, and then run off giggling like preteens with a secret crush. "You were with the air-headed blonde and the—"

"That's Jessica, my best friend. She's not an airhead, just slightly extroverted. She's the one who gets the box o' fun you carried out here. We figured somebody might as well get some use out of my discount."

A mixture of embarrassment, sorrow and yearning crossed her features when she made that confession. She wasn't getting any. No wonder her body had been so responsive to him.

This dual personality of hers was making him insane. One minute she blushed at a picture of a dildo and the next she pulled out the nearest one and got busy at her desk. She was like a virginal dominatrix, a hell of an erotic combination.

He'd taken the vibrator from her as a joke, but when he had seen the way passion clouded her eyes and her skin shivered at the slightest touch, he'd been well on his way to finding out how she would react to more. Much more. Good thing that party hadn't been planned for five minutes later or his sister would have caught him with his pants down—literally.

"Anyway, look, Evan. My friends thought a little casual sex would take my mind away from Jeff for a while. But the fact is—"

She stopped, her brows furrowed. He waited for what seemed like a year, wondering what awful thing was going to come out of her mouth. Finally she met his eyes again. "The fact is, it didn't do anything for me. I mean, what's the point of casual sex if you don't even get an orgasm out of it, right?"

Ouch.

The heat that had collected in his veins ran ice cold. Sleeping with him hadn't made her uncomfortable—she'd been *bored*. And he hadn't even noticed.

She needn't worry about his cockiness anymore. His ego had just dropped so low it was practically underground.

"Bree, I—"

"So, now you know." She cut him off and opened the driver's side door. "See you Monday."

She got in the car and drove off before he could respond. She was good at that.

He sighed and made his way back to the office, mentally kicking his own ass with every step. He had to make it up to her, but he didn't have time to form a plan because the second he walked in the door, Paula leveled him with an irritated look.

"I know you aren't hitting on my assistant a week into the job."

He crinkled his brow. "What? Who told you that?"

"I heard Lacy and Michelle chatting in the hallway. Apparently you're the hottest thing since sliced bread." An amused smile tugged at the corner of her mouth, softening her expression.

It sounded like the younger women were generating their own fantasized version of the story. He shook his head. "I'm not hitting on anybody. She asked me to go partying with her this weekend, so I figured I would go. It's been a while since I've been in town and I thought I might meet some people."

"Some girls, you mean."

"Smart. That's why they pay you the big bucks." What she didn't know was that he hoped going out and meeting people would take his mind off Bree. She'd been too distracting for his peace of mind even before she had made him feel like a bumbling middle-school kid who'd felt up his girlfriend and completely missed the target.

Paula smirked. "If you'll recall, now I pay *you* the big bucks."

"Yes, ma'am," he drawled in his best impression of a Southern accent. "Listen, I was thinking—have you considered opening an actual store in town?"

His sister's characteristic jabbering stopped, and she lowered her voice even though they were alone. "Of course I have. But I'll only be working another two weeks, and I won't have the energy to be messing with a project of that magnitude in between chemo treatments."

"Two weeks?" His heart sank. "I thought you weren't starting that for another two *months*."

"Well, I saw my doctor and apparently the cancer's showing signs of spreading. He wants me to get started as soon as possible. I told him I have to wrap things up here first."

She stared at the ground, and he reached forward to squeeze the tension from her shoulders. Paula's doctors believed her chances of making a full recovery were high, but regardless of their optimism, she'd been terrified since the day she heard her diagnosis.

"Hey, everything's going to be fine. I can handle this place."

"Just remember the deal, Evan. Everybody respects you or it's a no-go."

Like he'd forget. He had to impress all the employees because at the end of this trial period, Paula planned to hand out comment cards like she owned a restaurant and he was the new daily special.

He groaned just thinking about it. "You're not seriously going through with that awful survey idea, are you?"

"You better believe I am. I'm serious about this, Evan. This place, these people...this is my dream. I value my employees too much to leave them with a new boss they go home cursing about every day. I've got plenty of backup résumés if you don't make the grade."

"What makes you think they don't curse about you now?"

"Ha."

"I know the deal, sis. We all seem to be getting along so far. And considering I've already left my last job, I intend to keep it that way."

At least, he hoped so. A certain web designer was turning out to be much more difficult to win over than he thought she'd be.

Paula glared at him. "You quit? You know you're not getting promoted until I give everybody the news about my health, as well as my notice. Assuming things work out with you being here."

"They'll work out."

She waved her brightly painted fingernails. "Fine. Now get out of here, it's Friday night. Have a great birthday, and don't forget to lock up."

She breezed out the door, leaving Evan to contemplate the company's chances of profiting from a physical location. Customers would appreciate the absence of shipping costs and the ability to see and feel what they were buying, but there would also be drawbacks. Paula's business enjoyed overwhelming popularity because through the Web, she offered what many people wanted but were too afraid to admit in public—sex. Fun, unbridled lovemaking. At PPH, they got their chance to have it without sacrificing anonymity or breaking social norms.

He wished he had the same luxury. Being anonymous would have been nice a few minutes ago when Bree had pounded his last ounce of testosterone into the pavement. Clearly, she had a sensual side he'd been completely unaware of. The written content on the website aimed to excite visitors who weren't sufficiently convinced by the erotic photos. Paula wanted every visitor to leave a customer, and Bree's steamy records of how each item could be put to use were more than capable of accomplishing that goal.

She had plainly stated that he hadn't satisfied her, and he couldn't live with that. Not only was it an insult to his manhood, but an unsatisfied lover wouldn't have anything nice to say on the dumb survey that would make or break his future—and his promise to Tony.

Well, then. She didn't have a sex life at the moment, and he needed her acceptance to secure the CEO position. He knew at least one plan of action that would meet both of those needs—and this time, he wouldn't come like a teenage kid.

Chapter Four

Friday nights at Barry's were notorious for bringing together lustful men and scantily-dressed women. Plenty of both prowled the club tonight, eagerly searching for that special someone to share...maybe fifteen or twenty minutes. Once again, Bree found herself confined in a tiny booth with Jessica, Lynn and Tara-Beth.

At least this time she wore clothing that hid the body parts she preferred to keep covered. Her skirt showed plenty of leg but stopped short of revealing her rear end to everyone in sight. The form-fitting camisole accentuated her ample chest but kept it obscured from view, unlike the prostitute-inspired leather dress she'd reluctantly worn on The Night She Lost Her Mind.

She couldn't say the same for Jessie, whose not-quite-C cups spilled out of a scarlet V-neck dress thanks to a new push-up bra. Despite their ten-year age difference, Jess and Paula would get along beautifully, if their similar wardrobes were any indication.

Not that Bree wanted to spend much time thinking about Paula, because thoughts of Evan inevitably followed. She didn't know what disturbed her more—their charged encounter in her office, or the fact that it was midnight, and he and Michelle could be in an even more compromising position at that very moment.

She didn't know why she wanted him, but she was certain

she had to stop. She and Evan slung mud better than presidential candidates, and for all they had in common, they might as well hail from different planets. The scene at her desk had proven that acting on her attraction now would be an even bigger mistake than sleeping with him the first time. Then, she hadn't known what she was getting into. This time she had no excuse. He was pompous and promiscuous—everything she *didn't* want in a man—and there were dozens of ways to demonstrate her adventurous side without giving in to his charm. What, then, explained the ill feeling that congealed in her stomach when she pictured Evan's hands on Michelle—and the throbbing ache that bloomed between her legs when she imagined his hands on *her?*

A bored-looking server approached their table and offered a cocktail to Lynn, along with a folded paper napkin from the bar with something scribbled on the inside.

"From the guy in the black shirt," he intoned, his eyelids heavy with the weight of the umpteenth alcoholic gift he'd delivered that evening.

He made a quick escape, and Bree frowned at his rudeness. "That's helpful. There are a million guys in here wearing black shirts."

"Ooh!" Jessica shrieked. "A secret admirer! What does it say, what does it say?" She rubbed her palms together, the pink tip of her tongue sticking out in contrast against her red lips.

Lynn dragged the ends of the napkin apart, the playful grin on her face revealing her enjoyment of the suspense.

"That'll be enough of *that*," Jess cried. She stole the note away long enough to rip it open before Lynn snatched it back.

"I believe this delivery was for me," she said, wagging a finger at Jessica. "It says...boxers."

"Boxers?" the other girls exclaimed in unison.

Bree reached across the table and took the note, inspecting

it with a long swallow of her margarita. "What does that mean?"

"I don't—" Lynn's voice cut off as Jessica gasped and grabbed her arm. "What? *What?*"

Jess leaned over and whispered something in her ear. They erupted with laughter.

Bree exchanged a glance with Tara-Beth, who shrugged. "Uh, you guys—"

Lynn clapped her hand excitedly over Bree's mouth. "That's the question I asked the night you went home with him!"

She twisted her face away from Lynn's fingers. "What? Who?"

"Evan!"

Tara-Beth caught on and joined Lynn and Jessica in an unabashed stare at something of interest amidst the swarm of gyrating dancers. Knowing she would regret it, Bree looked anyway.

Sure enough, there stood Evan Willett. In the same room.

Again.

He lounged by the bar, once more looking the part of the tough, nonchalant playboy. His hair was more mussed than he wore it at work. A black T-shirt hugged the curves of every muscle on his upper body, and what a simple pair of jeans did to that *butt*—

Oh, my. She wasn't sure she was still breathing, but she was definitely gaping at him. One of his hands held a beer, the other gestured as he explained something to Michelle.

Michelle.

Ugh. Lacy had said they were going dancing.

Of course, they would go to Barry's. Of course, on the rare night she would be there to watch in agony.

"Who's that?" Tara-Beth asked, apparently noticing the girl at the same time Bree did.

"She's my boss's secretary."

"No way," Jessica said. "Can't he get in trouble for that?"

Bree shrugged. "*He's* not her boss. But I don't know that he'd care if he were."

Because he only cares about one thing, and she's got the anatomy to give it to him.

A waitress stopped at the end of the table and held out a martini, smiling at Tara-Beth. "From one of our patrons at the bar."

Four mouths dropped open. Tara-Beth accepted the drink and accompanying napkin, and Bree could see the note bore the same scrawled manuscript as Lynn's had. Evan's handwriting.

"Holy..." Tara-Beth let out a low whistle. "Bree, are you sure it was that bad?"

"What do you mean? What does it say?"

"I asked him what his favorite position was—"

"Tara!"

She smiled guiltily. "It says, 'the one where I can see her face when she comes apart at my touch'. The word *comes* is underlined."

The table fell quiet. Lynn put her hand over her heart. Jessica fanned herself with a menu.

Tara-Beth held up the note to prove she spoke the truth. Bree glanced at Evan again, but he was yapping with a group of guys huddled around one of the televisions at the bar.

"You guys can't actually believe that. The man is a robot, I'm telling you." But her skin burned under her skirt, and she recalled the look in his eyes when he had put that vibrator to her leg. Unlike six months ago, he'd been focused on her reactions. He'd been focused on her, period.

Three or four rounds, he'd said the other day. Oh, what she would give for just one.

She refused to think about it any longer. Her priorities did not include becoming one of Evan's groupies or falling into the trap of believing she was important to him just because they'd slept together. *She* associated sex with significance. He probably marked his numerous quickies on his headboard.

She turned back to her friends. "Didn't he answer any of your questions the night you actually talked to him?"

"Only when we asked him if he was single, and he said yes," Lynn replied between bites of a French fry. "After that, he just kind of looked at us funny."

"Imagine that."

Jessica sipped her frozen concoction and made a sour face when it struck her with brain freeze. When she recovered, she stated, "Wow, I hope he answers my question."

Bree closed her eyes. "Dare I ask what it was?"

"I just asked him if he thought you were cute."

Well, that wasn't so bad. She wouldn't mind getting that one answered. It would be nice to know if he'd slept with her simply because she was a female or if he had actually found her attractive.

And if he still did.

Sure enough, when about five minutes had passed, the original waiter returned with Jessica's drink. "You ladies are popular tonight," he commented, not looking nearly as bored when Jessica flipped her wavy blonde hair over her shoulder and flashed him a demure smile.

Bree tried to pay attention to the conversation at the table, but she couldn't pull her gaze away from Evan and whatever game he was playing with her. Michelle stood at the bar, looking annoyed while he danced with another girl.

"Ma'am?"

Blinking, she turned her attention to the beckoning waiter. "This one's for you," he claimed.

Her throat felt like a bowling ball had gotten stuck there. Shakily, she thanked the younger man and wrapped both of her hands around the heavy, bowl-shaped glass to avoid dropping it. Strawberry daiquiri—her favorite. She'd been drinking it the night they met. She looked at the crimson-colored ice and his words from the previous day echoed in her ears: *Red is definitely your color.*

She'd gone insane with the need to prove she wasn't shy and conservative. Not quite brave enough to smack that condescending look off his face, she'd let him look down her shirt instead. It would have been degrading if he hadn't been so obviously turned on.

"Well?" Jessica asked impatiently. "What does your note say?"

"Read yours first."

Jessie cleared her throat and unfolded her napkin. "It says—" She stopped. A warm smile lit her features.

Bree waited, dying of anticipation. "What?"

"She's beautiful."

Lynn and Tara-Beth gasped, emitting little sounds of appreciation. Bree looked down at her own folded note, her lungs tight with disbelief. "Are you sure these are from Evan? This doesn't sound like him at all."

Jessica grinned while she fluttered her fingers in Evan's direction. "Maybe that's the point."

The wave didn't bypass Bree's watchful gaze. "He's looking at us?"

"He's looking at you. Open yours. Now."

She sighed and leaned back against the booth, disappointment seeping into her gut. "You're right, it is the point. These notes aren't sincere. He's doing this because I told him he didn't give me an orgasm."

Her friends stared at her like she'd jumped on top of the bar and performed a striptease. She knew without a doubt they were shocked because she'd said the word "orgasm" to a man. Maybe she was making progress, after all.

Jessica hooted. "Look at you, moving right down that list!"

"That's on the list?"

"Number two. Talking dirty. I'd say telling a man he didn't put his money where his mouth is—or his mouth where something else was—"

Tara-Beth jumped in. "What she's trying to say is, it counts."

Jessica's smile widened. "Yeah. Damn, I'm proud of you! What inspired you to do that?"

"He wanted to know why I left his place that night. This guy's criticizing my job performance, remember? What was I supposed to say? 'Getting naked with a stranger made me want to throw up' wouldn't exactly make me sound like an expert on sexual fantasy."

Lynn leaned forward. "You know what this means, don't you? If he's using these notes to try to make it up to you, you've found your man."

"The man to help you complete the list," Jessica clarified, still grinning. "Now open that note!"

Bree did, her heart sounding like the Kentucky Derby in her ears. Sometimes she felt like everyone in the world had experienced the fun on that list, and she ached to join them without racking up a huge list of partners. If Evan wanted to make something up to her, she could let him think he was doing her a favor. He'd never have to know she could count on one finger the number of other men who'd touched her.

"Will you excuse me for a sec?" She clambered out of the booth with the napkin in her fist. "And whatever you do, don't let him leave."

Evan had aimed to win Bree's affection with his maze of allusive notes, but when she opened the napkin and ran off to the bathroom instead of into his arms like he'd imagined, he reluctantly turned his attention back to Michelle.

She hadn't caught any of the hints he'd dropped to let her know their relationship wasn't going beyond that of friends. When she'd asked him out that afternoon, he had seen a social opportunity, something he'd never been quick to turn down. There hadn't been any dinner or picking her up at her place. He'd simply met her at Barry's for a quick drink.

Michelle, however, seemed to believe the night constituted a date at the very least. Despite his purposeful moves to dance with other women and fraternize with everyone sitting around the bar, she refused to leave his side.

He'd planned to stick it out and break the news to her at the end of the night, but then Bree Jamison had walked through the door, surrounded by the same group of girls from before and looking a thousand times more sophisticated than them or anyone else in the place. The busty blonde at her side resembled the type of woman he usually approached for a casual evening, but he'd been drawn to Bree since day one. He couldn't tear his eyes or his thoughts away from her.

So she had taken care of the problem for him by disappearing into the restroom. Unfortunately, only a riled girl determined to have things her way remained in his line of vision.

"Hey, Evan," Michelle gushed. "My roommate's out of town and I've got the place to myself tonight. Would you like to come by for a while?"

Roommate? Oh, Lord. Either she was really young or he was too damn old, because a decade had passed since he'd known anyone who lived with a roommate.

She gazed up at him with an adoring smile that told him she'd give it up in the middle of the club if he wanted. She was very attractive, but too young, too naive...too easy. He liked the chase. Surely that explained his obsession with Bree, who had been running from him—literally—since their first meeting.

He gritted his teeth and put great effort into not pulling away when Michelle dragged her fingernails down his arm. "Actually, I'm thinking about calling it a night. It's been a long week."

"Well..." Snaking her arm around his waist, she continued, "I guess I can settle for a goodnight kiss."

"Michelle." He stepped out of her reach and plunked his beer glass down on the bar. "I really need to tell you—"

"Wow, we've all had a long week, haven't we?" An airy laugh drifted into his ears, and he turned to find Bree standing next to him, gesturing at the three PPH employees and their drinks.

Awareness of her body and its proximity to his washed over him, and the entire surface of his skin came alive. "Bree, what a surprise. I was just telling Michelle the same thing."

She gave her colleague a friendly smile, but Michelle returned the greeting with a distracted nod. "Hey, Bree."

"Listen, Evan, I have a quick question that can't wait until Monday. Can I see you for a second?"

"Sure," he answered, though he could practically see storm clouds brewing over her head. His clever note tactic was about to backfire, but he wasn't going to pass up an opportunity to be alone with her. At least, as alone as two people could be in this jam-packed room of sweaty people.

He said goodbye to Michelle, leaving her at the bar after she insisted he didn't need to see her out. Then he wormed his way through the crowd and joined Bree near the front entrance. As he'd suspected she would, she dropped her angelic façade.

"What is this?" She thrust the note closer to his nose with each word.

It dangled in front of him, where he could read his handwritten plea for another chance. *Would you have stayed if I'd remembered to kiss you?*

It was pathetic, but true. He had only realized it today after she'd told him exactly what a horrible lover he'd been, but he hadn't even kissed her. He'd nibbled a bit of her neck, made his way down to her collarbone, but not once had he tasted that beautiful mouth. Their quickie had happened at light speed. He couldn't believe his balls were still attached after such a crude display of selfishness. That wasn't his definition of a man.

What had put him in such a rush? He'd always avoided falling into the married-with-children trap that sent his parents to the poorhouse and eventually divorce court, but he knew enough to put a lady first in the bedroom, no matter how brief the affair. Not to mention his refusal to commit to more than a night had never sent women running before. He'd known some to hang on until he ended the sex out of exhaustion. One thing was certain—when he met Bree, he'd entered uncharted territory.

He studied the note as though seeing it for the first time. "It looks like a question. You should answer it."

She pressed her lips together. "This isn't necessary. I'm sorry I was rude to you earlier. Like I said, that night was just a stupid—"

"Bet? Decision? Yeah, I get that. But if I hadn't shown the self-control of a fifteen-year-old, maybe you would have gotten over him."

Though she tried to keep a straight face, a smile threatened as she mulled over his suggestion. "I'm over him."

"Are you?"

"Yes. And thanks for the drinks. My friends think you're practically a god."

"They're pretty smart, then."

"Ha, ha." She combed her hand through her hazel-streaked locks, fidgeting like a shy teenager on a first date. "Look, I just wanted to thank you for the compliments, if that's what they were. I imagine we'll be able to work together now without killing each other."

She offered him a brief, tender smile, then headed toward the door. Just as he was about to give in to the overwhelming urge to call her back, she tossed a coy glance over her shoulder. "If you want to discuss this further, I wouldn't mind an escort back to my car."

Oh, sweet heaven. If he remembered correctly, her car had dark tinted windows, which made it a good place to discuss anything. Especially missed opportunities for searing kisses and mind-blowing sex.

Without hesitation, he followed her.

Chapter Five

Michelle trudged up the stairs that led to her second-floor apartment, wishing she could blame her misery on too many drinks at the club. She'd prefer to spend tonight drowning in alcohol, or better yet, Evan's bed sheets. Instead, she was choking on her own stupidity. As usual.

The gum she'd been chewing to freshen her breath in case of traffic cops had gone tasteless. She pulled the wad out of her mouth and dropped it over the side of the staircase, then pounded on her neighbor's door.

"Harry, get your ass over here! I need help."

His door squeaked open. Though she had her back turned while she fumbled with her lock, she could hear the sneer in his voice. "Why, pray tell, do I always have to come to your place when *you* are the one who needs help?"

"Because your place smells like a sewage plant." She jammed her key into the knob and twisted it open. This evening had been a royal screw-up, and she wasn't in the mood for his stupid remarks.

Harry—or Hairy, as she liked to think of him due to the excess of the stuff on his hands and chin—laughed and followed her inside, heading straight for the four inches of space that served as her kitchen. "I'm guessing you didn't get laid."

She growled. "What are you, a Mensa member? Do you see

a man here?"

"I can't help you if you don't give me any details about your seduction of the new boy."

"It didn't go exactly as I'd hoped." Understatement of the century.

He found a bottle of vodka and helped himself to a glass. "Apparently not. You look like you've got a serious case of blue...tits."

She rolled her eyes when he started cackling again. Harry was annoying as hell, a gamer who supported himself with online poker winnings and only braved sunlight when he had to go to the convenience store for toilet paper—and even that was questionable. She put up with him because he was nauseatingly smart and had bailed her out of trouble more times than she cared to admit.

"Will you shut it? I'll come up with another plan." She had to. She was in way over her head. Her latest attempt to improve her life was shaping up like an episode of Jerry Springer, and if she didn't fix things fast, innocent people would get hurt.

Paula's hot brother's appearance at the office yesterday had seemed like the answer to her prayers. She hadn't counted on him being so uncooperative at the club—and having Bree show up, when Evan obviously wanted to get into her pants, had not helped.

"Okay, so you can't date Mr. Cool. What are you going to do now?" Harry poked at his gums with a toothpick and then twirled it around in his drink.

Michelle watched him, disgusted. "I can see why you don't have any friends. You're bizarre."

"I have you."

"Not for long, at the rate you're going."

He downed the vodka in one swallow and released a

pungent sigh in her direction. "Lucky for you, I spent a lot of time today thinking about your dilemma, and I have an idea."

Hands waving in dramatic gestures, he explained what he'd come up with in great detail. If she understood him right, he would do most of the dirty work and she'd sweep in at the last minute to save the day...and a few careers. Possibly a marriage. And definitely her own ass.

This was the reason she continued to subject herself to Harry's obnoxious comments and toxic hygiene. He could transform her from an orphaned dropout who made a few bucks an hour to a fucking superhero in a couple of weeks' time.

Her despair lifted. "That just might work."

"Of course it will." He crossed his arms and leaned against her refrigerator. "So, has my genius convinced you to spend the night with me? For you, I'd even clean up the place."

She snorted. Over the three years they'd lived across the hall from each other, she had never gotten him out of her apartment without hearing him beg for sex. He couldn't get it anywhere else unless he fed his credit card number to a porn site.

"Keep dreaming," she replied. "We've already had this discussion. I don't sleep with friends."

"I see. You prefer men who are utterly unavailable."

She pointed at the door, hoping he would move in that direction. "I'll worry about my personal life, and you worry about yours. That is, if you ever get one."

"Touché. How about this? You do me a favor after I bail you out of the biggest mess you've ever gotten into. Otherwise, that fabulous plan will slip my mind."

"Is that a threat?"

"It's my final offer. I'm tired of not getting anything out of everything I do for you."

"So don't do it," she snapped.

He lifted his shoulders. "Your call." Tossing his toothpick into her sink, he headed for the door.

Panic surged through her. Damn it, that man knew how to run her into a corner. "Wait!" she called, grabbing his arm seconds before he slammed the door on her chance at redemption.

He turned, a smug smile on his face. "Yes?"

"Fine. You've got a deal. Now get busy."

Standing outside Barry's with Evan beside her and a soft breeze teasing her feverish skin, Bree realized she didn't have the slightest idea how to begin a no-holds-barred seduction.

They ambled down the sidewalk, following the moonlit concrete to a line of cars parallel-parked on the side of the street. She had about as much experience downtown in the middle of the night as she did with one-night stands, but she felt safe with a brawny man by her side. Though she had to admit, getting mugged wasn't the first thing on her mind. Instead, visions of walking hand-in-hand with Evan danced in her
head—walking hand-in-hand through a field of sunflowers to the tune of cheesy background music.

She stifled a giggle at the ridiculous image. Somehow, between his eyebrow ring and the tattoo she couldn't help wondering about because her mental picture included his naked skin, Evan didn't seem like the flowers and soft music type.

"I haven't said anything yet."

She blinked and looked up at him. "What?"

"You're laughing." He almost looked hurt.

"No, I was—never mind. I'm sorry. Go ahead." Maybe she should put a leash on her newly-liberated hormones. He was attempting a decent conversation with her while she dreamed of romantic walks and tried to set up another roll in his bed. She'd spent more time primping in the bathroom at Barry's than she had during the moments before her first interview with Paula, and she had never wanted anything more than she had that day...until now.

Evan stopped walking and turned to face her, his expression serious. "I didn't write those notes so we could work together without killing each other. I wrote them because I wanted to tell you—"

An onslaught of honking and shouting interrupted him as a car full of teenagers whizzed past. In a flash, Evan grabbed her and held her against his chest, though the car wasn't anywhere near the sidewalk. Her cheek brushed his shirt, and she tried not to gasp her need as the scent and feel of him surrounded her.

The urge to kiss him grew irresistible. She shifted in his arms and moved to do so, but he put some space between them, his eyes trained on the car racing down the street.

"Are you okay?" he asked.

She hadn't been hit by a car, if that's what he wanted to know. But if *okay* meant calm and collected and not in desperate need of his touch, then she was seriously hurt.

"I'm fine. What did you want to tell me?"

She gave herself a mental pat on the back. Good answer. More talking, less touching. And absolutely no more sudden protective moves that would make her want to jump him—at least, not until she figured out how to get him back in bed to help her tackle that list.

"I screwed up that night," he said. "I know we were only in it for fun, but you deserved more than the three minutes I gave you. I'm sorry for being such a prick."

Stunned, she met his eyes. There was no trace of ridicule on his face, no sarcasm in his voice. His expression remained sincere, and for the first time, she recognized him as a man with feelings instead of a heartless character out of her melodramatic love life.

His apology crumbled what was left of her guard. "You're nothing at all like I thought."

He looked amused. "What did you think?"

"Well, you know." She squirmed. "The eyebrow thing. I thought you were some kind of punk."

"A punk."

"Yeah."

"And you slept with me?"

She laughed, well aware of how foolish that seemed. "You looked dangerous. I thought you were macho. I was attracted to that."

The admission came out too fast, before she remembered she was supposed to be convincing him she'd done it all—even with "dangerous" men. They arrived at her car, and she fell silent so as not to say anything else that would make her sound weak.

He paused before responding. "And the Jeff guy—he wasn't enough of a man for you?"

"Jeff had no imagination. I guess that's good for someone who's into science and medicine. But he was...mechanical."

The very same thing she'd complained regarding Evan. How wrong she was turning out to be.

"Tell me how mechanical this is."

He took her face in his hands and secured his mouth over hers. Her jaw opened to release a shocked gasp, and he deepened the kiss. The flavor of lager on his tongue mingled with the hint of strawberry on hers. She clung to him for another taste, longing to soothe the hunger inside her.

When his fingers massaged a slow path through her hair, she considered enjoying a life of physical pleasure and disregarding that whole marriage and family thing. It didn't seem all that important while his careful strokes swept her mouth, engaging in a deliberate exploration that ignited the embers hidden away behind years of self-control. Surely such a soft caress could not be coming from someone as obstinate as Evan. What had happened to the "robot" she remembered? This man was undeniably human, his gentle lips plying hers even as an ample erection made itself known through the denim pressed against her hip.

"Evan..." She tried to object to groping each other in the middle of the sidewalk, wanting badly to collapse on a warm, soft bed and entangle her every limb with his. But her voice sounded tiny in the wake of his touch and the million butterflies it sent fluttering through her veins.

He released her lips just long enough to reply, "Don't say anything." Then he possessed her mouth again, and she had to admit, she didn't feel like talking, either. Her legs melted beneath her.

A catcall rang out, jolting them apart.

"Woo-hoo!"

"Get a room!"

Hysterical laughter came from the same rowdy kids who had passed them in the car. The group crossed the street, undoubtedly on their way to another club.

"Bree, give me your keys."

"What? I only drank—"

Evan swiped them from her hand and unlocked her sedan, then gallantly opened the back door.

She eyed him. "What are you doing?"

"Getting us a room."

"Are you crazy?"

He wrapped an arm around her waist and leaned close to her ear. "Five minutes," he murmured. "You can't go your whole life without making out in a car."

She didn't need to ask how he knew she'd never done that. Hard as she tried to look the part of the racy, adventurous woman who sold sex toys for a living, on the inside she was still the innocent girl he'd witnessed at his apartment. She did have the missionary romps with Jeff, but those plain-Jane experiences didn't seem to count. She had a feeling Evan could teach her things that would make her cry—with pleasure. Maybe even scream.

And when he gave her a slow, sultry grin and his brow ring flashed in the amber light of the street lamp, she really, *really* wanted to learn.

Still, though, she hardly knew him and—

"You know, it isn't rocket science." With a look that said her contemplation time was up, he practically tackled her into the car.

"Hey!" she screeched, but she was laughing.

He closed and locked the door after them. "This," he said, brushing a strand of hair from her forehead, "is what I meant to do at my apartment."

The joke over, he met her gaze, his eyes as dark and fierce as brewing storm clouds. She shivered. Was that what desire looked like? Jeff had never looked at her like that. No one had.

Evan's hands braced both sides of her waist, and the storm hit. His lips met hers with a tender aggression that pressed her against the seat. Electricity shook her from head to toe, making her every hair stand on end. She moved her tongue with his and fisted her fingers in his soft, dark hair. His clothing brushed against her, tying her stomach in knots, increasing her sense of awareness a hundredfold. Their bodies were so close, so ready to continue the sensual frenzy until they were joined.

If she didn't know better, she would never believe this guy could get off without thinking of anything beyond a small space between her legs. With only a kiss and the stirring sensation of his fingertips grazing the edge of her shirt, he worked her body like a man who could make love for hours and make sure she enjoyed every minute of it.

The idea turned her bones to putty. He ran one hand across her abdomen and dipped his thumb lightly inside her navel, then dropped his head beneath her chin and licked the swell of her breast which peeked out from the neckline of her top. Goose bumps rose all over her skin. She clutched at his head when he kissed her again, crushing his body to hers so she could feel his arousal straining against her thigh.

A loud rap sounded on the window above her head, and they both jumped. The sudden separation of Evan's lips from hers stung like a ripped-off bandage. She turned to see a purple-haired teenager making obscene gestures on the other side of the door.

Evan bolted from the car, and Bree couldn't help but grin while he fed the kid and his groupies a few choice words that sent them running to the other side of the street. At least his tough-guy side was good for something.

"Damn kids," he grumbled when he rejoined her in the seat. "Another reason no one will catch me raising them."

He reached for her again, no doubt ready to finish what they'd started, but she took his arms and held him a few inches away from her. "You don't want kids? Ever?"

"Hell, no. I know what you're thinking and don't worry about it. I've got condoms. Plenty of them."

Her hopes for a heated night with him deflated like a punctured balloon. She wanted badly to give in to her need and forget about the consequences, but how could she make love with a man who despised everything she dreamed of having someday?

Granted, it was supposed to be cheap sex. She was supposed to be going through Jessica's list and *practicing* for the man she'd marry, not acting as though Evan were that man. But years of believing in sex as every bit an emotional connection as a physical one didn't go away that easily.

"I can't do this."

Evan sat back in disbelief, his sensitive moment apparently over. "How do you expect me to give you an orgasm if you don't let me touch you?"

She straightened in the seat, hurt by his sour tone. "Is that what this was all about?"

"You told me I didn't satisfy you, and I'm admitting you're right. I'm trying to make it up to you."

"Well, let me give you a piece of advice. You can't give a woman what she wants without paying attention to more than her body."

"I've done it plenty of times before."

Without a doubt, Ego Man was back. Why on earth had she let him kiss her? "Maybe they were faking it."

His derisive stare made her look away.

Okay. So her pebble-tipped breasts had poked into his chest, and her legs shook with the effort to keep her knees together and hide the moisture that would make her attraction to him all too obvious. He was good, much better than she'd given him credit for the first time. But one thing hadn't changed—when they were together, he focused on sex for the sake of sex. As much as she wanted to expand her horizons, she wasn't okay with being little more than a blow-up doll with a heart rate.

A shiver traveled down her spine and doused the warmth caused by his momentary tenderness. She'd felt so cheap and used and dirty when she had discovered how easily Jeff had jumped into bed with another woman. Sleeping with Evan would be voluntarily putting herself through that again. He'd just admitted that he viewed women as outlets for his sexual frustration. As soon as he was done with her, he'd move right on to the next girl.

Disgusted, and fed up with trying to have casual sex when she obviously couldn't do it, she exited the car. "I think I'd like to go home now. Goodbye."

Evan followed suit, crossing his arms and pushing his lips together. "Your whole image is fake, then. You really are a prude."

She ignored the sting of his words, vowing to become the world's most valuable employee over the next couple of weeks. If she couldn't change Evan's mind about her without signing up for another course in heartache, she'd have to impress Paula so much that his opinion wouldn't be enough to thwart a job offer.

"I said, goodbye." She moved to the driver's seat and slammed the door, loudly playing the stereo until he walked away.

Chapter Six

"Tell me this isn't happening. Tell me my life did not just end."

Bree looked over her shoulder at Todd and waited for a response to her desperate plea. He leaned forward, inspecting the empty space on the website where his Bath Buddy photo should have resided. It had disappeared over the weekend, along with her content. The entire page was missing.

Not a good start to her campaign for Best Employee Ever. At this rate, Paula could fire her before Evan even had a chance to blab that she didn't have the sexual knowledge necessary to work there.

"That's really strange." Todd adjusted his glasses and peered more closely at the vacant screen, his voice unusually cross.

Bristling, Bree did her best to stop her fist from clobbering the top of her desk. The vandalism of her work was more than strange. It was deliberate.

"Everything was fine when I left on Friday, so hopefully it hasn't been down too long. The individual files are still in their original condition. I'll just stick it all back up." She didn't feel nearly as confident as she sounded.

Her website wasn't having technical difficulties. All the pages loaded fine except for the one displaying PPH's current promotion. Someone had purposely deleted the information from the new Bath Buddy page, leaving a blank screen to greet interested customers, who had most likely lost interest after seeing the problem and bought their items somewhere else.

She felt ill at the realization that only one person other than her and Todd knew where to find those web files. That person had kissed her Friday night.

And walked away angry with her.

Surely Evan wouldn't mess with her work because she had stopped their childish make-out session. He wouldn't want to damage his own sister's company...but maybe he hadn't thought of it that way. Maybe he had only focused on making Bree look bad.

"I don't know what to tell you," Todd said, straightening up with a shake of his head. "I'd say fix what you can and we'll talk to Paula about it later today. I don't think it's a major emergency. Like you said, it couldn't have been gone but a day or so."

Exactly. Saturday and Sunday, the most profitable days of the week. Their site wasn't the type people could log onto at work without serious consequences, so weekends saw a lot of traffic. If Paula noticed a substantial drop in sales resulting from the outage, the blame would land directly on Bree. Responsibility for maintaining the site fell squarely on her shoulders.

Evan knew that.

"Knock, knock."

He leaned against the door frame, back in his professional, non-black duds. He and Todd nodded as they passed each other, and Evan sat in a chair next to her desk.

"How's it going?" he asked casually.

She didn't return the greeting, though her insides did flips at the sight of his virile body and the memory of being entwined around it in the backseat of her car. "You didn't do any work on the website over the weekend, did you?"

"Over the weekend? Hell, no. I don't like my sister *that* much."

She felt no impulse to laugh at the joke. The knowledge that someone had dug around in her files unnerved her. And Evan's jovial attitude was entirely out of place after their argument.

Maybe he's playing nice so I won't suspect him.

He leaned down and peered under her desk.

"What are you doing?"

He glanced up at her like she should know the answer to that question. "Um, I'm looking for that thing we dropped on Friday afternoon. Before Paula or someone else comes in and thinks you've been having a grand old time in here behind closed doors."

She cursed. "Hurry up and get it before somebody comes in. My door's open."

"I think someone already took care of it for us." He sat back up.

"What do you mean?"

"It's not there."

Her heart skipped a beat before she remembered the cleaning service that came in every night. "Oh. Well, the housekeeping lady—or man—probably had a grand old time this weekend."

Evan made a face. "Nice. And speaking of weekends, how was yours?"

She caught the swagger in his tone. No doubt, he was referring to their unfortunate lip-lock. "Gloating, are we?"

"Not at all. I found it very enjoyable."

If that kiss was just *enjoyable*, Antarctica was just a really big ice cube. But no way would she let him know how hard he'd rocked her world. "Uh-huh. About as enjoyable as the six million other people you've kissed this month."

"Give me some credit, will you? I am capable of looking at women as individuals."

"Can you prove that?"

"I bet I can."

"Yeah, well, I think I'll pass." She shuffled some papers, clueless about the content of any of them. "The last bet I took landed me in bed with you."

"Maybe this one will, too."

She threw the paperwork back on her desk and fixed him with an icy glare, trying hard to overlook the twinkling brown eyes and mischievous smile that rallied her lower body with each glimpse. "Will you knock it off? You know that's not going to happen."

He folded his arms over a chest she longed to see naked— not that it didn't look edible in the dress shirt he wore. "Why not? Because you're too good for me?"

Lacy stuck her head in the door, and they exchanged quick good mornings. When she was gone, Bree leaned back in her chair and crossed her legs. Guilt seeped into her gut.

"I never said that."

"You didn't have to. You're obviously a person who puts this huge significance on sex, and because I haven't been saving myself for some unrealistic notion of a lifelong relationship, you won't let me past first base no matter how much you want it."

His accurate interpretation of her actions left her dumbfounded. "It's not unrealistic. My parents have been married for almost forty years. Look at Todd. Look at—"

"Exceptions. They got lucky. My parents are separated and

have been since I was a kid. The point is, you're missing out on a hell of a good time. Why did you apply for this job if you're so afraid of sex?"

She opened her mouth, indignant, as he stood to leave. But first he bent down and said in her ear, "Stop fighting it, Miss Priss. You know you were getting hot in the car."

She wadded up an old document and launched it at him, but he exited too fast and the paper ball struck the next person entering her office—Paula.

"Oh!" She covered her mouth. "I'm so sorry. That wasn't aimed at you."

Paula plucked the weapon from the floor and gave her a wry smile. "Evan being his usual charming self?"

"It's not as bad as it seems. We don't usually resort to violence."

"Good, because I don't want any blood spilled on the new project I've got for you two."

Bree laughed, thankful that Paula hadn't come in to lecture her about the website. "Sounds interesting. What kind of project?"

"Evan and I were going over some new marketing approaches, and we've decided it's time to expand. You know, get some tangible things out there in addition to our online presence. The first order of business is a printed brochure."

Bree grabbed a legal pad and jotted down some notes. Concept-driven, colorful, directed at couples. She would need to discuss graphics with Todd.

Excitement pulsed through her. She'd hoped to get one more major assignment before the end of her contract, something she could pour her heart into perfecting and then clinch the full-time position. The brochure sounded like just the ticket.

When they'd hashed out the details, Paula gave her a wink. "Good luck. I know you can do this. I'd like to discuss your contract next week if that works for you."

"Absolutely."

Next week? She'd have the pamphlet done in the next *hour* if it meant Paula would reward her with the job. She scribbled a sticky note reminding her to talk to Evan about the project, though it wasn't likely she'd forget when he filled more of her mind with each passing day. Talking to him was all she wanted to do anymore, despite his penchant for offensive comments.

She was *not* afraid of sex. And what did he mean by "Miss Priss"? She wasn't stuck up. Sure, she preferred living on the affluent side of town. She valued certain traits like education, cleanliness, success...

Oh, no. She sounded like one of her mom's frequent lectures about the proper attributes of a husband. The next point out of the older woman's mouth would undoubtedly be something regarding the "trashiness" of people who drink, sleep around, and defile their bodies with things like tattoos and neon hair.

Did she really think she was better than Evan?

Maybe she had acted a little snobbish toward him. She'd insulted him at the airport and then invited him to her car Friday night with every intention of seducing him, only to wimp out because he didn't share her desire to have children. But what was she supposed to do? Even the new Bree wanted a family someday, and she couldn't accomplish that by falling for a guy who believed love was unrealistic. Her attraction to him was fast-growing and troublesome as a persistent weed, and she needed to kill it fast.

Between the vibrator incident and a few minutes in her backseat, she'd managed to cover a third of the list. Maybe that was enough. Her main reason for wanting more sexual experience had been to advance her career, and Paula had just handed her the final hurdle. If she cleared it, she was in.

She looked at the Post-It she'd written Evan's name on and crumpled it in her fist. She had to do this brochure, and do it right. Alone. Until she found out who was responsible for deleting the web page, she couldn't trust Evan around her work—and she couldn't trust herself around him.

Getting Bree naked had quickly earned a place at the top of Evan's "must do" list. He wanted to make love with her for a lot of reasons—to replace their bad memories with much better ones, to prove to her that orgasms and respect did not require commitment, to find out if her sexy side would stomp her modesty for good if he made her scream and moan in ecstasy.

She was so damned hot when she denied the past and their present desire for each other by pretending they were acquaintances with nothing to discuss outside of work. While they hovered over the conference table making plans for Paula's brochure, she fussed over her laptop computer and avoided his eyes at all costs. She kept her legs crossed, one bouncing furiously over the other, and those erect nipples begged him to unbutton her top and close his mouth right over one of them, then the other.

Oh, man. He needed a cold shower, but since that wouldn't be available until he returned home, a cold drink would have to do.

"Need anything?" he asked Bree, rising from his chair.

"No, thanks," she said to the computer.

In the break room, he scanned the fridge for possibilities, and Todd came in to refill his coffee mug. "Hey, Evan."

"What's up?"

"Did Bree tell you what happened over the weekend?"

Evan retrieved a Coke and made sure to wipe the grin off his face before he closed the refrigerator. He knew exactly what Bree had done over the weekend, but Todd probably wasn't talking about that. "No, what happened?"

"Somebody trashed our brand new product page. Took down the photos, the content, everything. It was totally blank when we got in this morning."

"We got hacked?" His high spirits dropped. Paula did not need this on top of everything else she had going on. "Does Paula know—"

"No, man. It wasn't a hacker. Somebody got into Bree's computer and took things off the page, one by one. Looks like an inside job."

Was that suspicion in Todd's eyes? He had to be kidding. Evan was tempted to inform his colleague that he would hardly try to sink PPH considering he'd be running it soon. But right then, Todd looked like he could easily get pissed off. And Evan had to play nice so the employees wouldn't pitch a fit over the change in management. *And* Paula didn't want her health news broadcast around the office yet.

In other words, he had no way to defend himself.

"No, she didn't say anything. I'll go talk to her about it."

The notion of some adolescent hacker poking around in their site had made him mad, but his anger boiled over when he imagined Bree spreading rumors all over the office that he was butchering her work. If Paula caught wind of that, she would take the job from under his nose in a heartbeat.

He wouldn't tolerate that. No matter how badly he wanted to sleep with Bree.

Every snide remark he could have made, though, slipped his mind when he walked back into the conference room and saw her sitting at the table, absorbed in her work. Since she didn't seem to know he was standing there, he paused in the doorway and surveyed her figure.

Her hair was pulled back from her face with a headband, and she chewed on the inside of her cheek while squinting into her computer screen. A smile threatened despite the problem on his mind. He moved his gaze down to admire her defined collarbone and the snug white shirt with a neckline that barely covered the top of her lush breasts. A loose black skirt draped to her knees, and pink-tipped toenails peeked out from shoes with heels so high he wasn't quite sure how she got around in them.

He preferred to think about how she got around without them. Or any other clothing, for that matter.

"Can I help you?"

Oops.

He dragged his attention away from pleasure and back to business. "Todd told me there was a problem with the website this morning."

Her expression darkened. "Yes. It appears someone wasn't happy with my Bath Buddy page. Since that happens to be our newest product and this month's promotion, greeting our customers with a blank page probably didn't help this weekend's sales."

The accusation in her tone rankled him. He had no idea what had happened to the website, but he did know that employees were turning on him left and right, and he had to change that. Fast.

More importantly, he had to patch things up with Bree. His job depended on it, not to mention his chances of getting closer to her outside the office were deteriorating at breakneck speed.

"Do you need help getting it back up?"

Well, that hadn't come out right. The steamy image that formed in his head had nothing to do with the website, and judging from the rosy shade of Bree's face, she'd pictured the exact same thing.

"The page, I mean," he corrected.

"I've already fixed it. Everything's fine, I just need to gather some more information for this brochure. Todd's getting a head start on the graphics and we should be able to send it to the printer within a couple of days."

"Why don't you take a breather? Give me what you've got, and I'll spend some time on it today and work on it from home tonight."

She snapped her laptop closed and got up from the table. "*I'll* work on it tonight," she said. "You just worry about getting a list of contacts together so we can send this stuff out as soon as possible."

She didn't trust him. This was getting worse by the minute, and his patience had reached its breaking point. He'd tried several times to get them on equal ground, but she refused to let go of that damned snooty attitude. They had worked together for several days now, and she knew that he was an intelligent human being capable of holding down a job. She knew he owned the nice clothes she considered so important, and she was well aware of their attraction to each other.

Despite all of that, she continued to treat him like the "punk" she'd pegged him in her deluded imagination. She didn't approach him like a professional, and it would probably kill her to consider him a friend. He'd been confronted with such prejudice in the past, and he hadn't put up with it then, either.

"I'll tell you what. Since you enjoy treating me like a three-year-old, why don't you show me to my room and I'll play with my toys."

"Will you just—"

"No, I understand. I'm obviously not capable of doing this kind of work. I went to public school, I wear jewelry, and my daddy isn't a hotshot lawyer."

"Evan!"

"I'll be at my desk trying to remember my alphabet. If your highness needs anything, you let me know."

Taking one last bittersweet look at her shocked eyes and open mouth, he stalked out of the conference room and slammed the door.

Chapter Seven

The box had been sitting in her lap for thirty minutes.

Bree sat cross-legged on the floor next to her desk. It was nine-thirty at night, and the only light in the entire suite shone from a dim lamp in the corner of her office. Everyone else had gone home hours ago. She had grabbed a bite to eat and then returned to continue working on the product brochures. She'd barely gotten anything done that day. She couldn't concentrate when Evan was under the same roof.

Especially when he was mad at her.

It had been easier in the empty office. Without any distractions, she'd written up a considerable amount of information within a couple of hours. Definitely enough for Todd to build a design around. Now, having finished working, she was alone with her thoughts—and the intriguing box she'd forgotten to deliver to Jessica.

While searching for a cable for her laptop after dinner, she'd discovered the package in her trunk and brought it inside with her. Maybe she could take one peek.

She shouldn't. The contents of Jessica's order could be very personal. Then again, knowing Jess, she would probably encourage Bree to jump right in and experiment to her heart's content. Maybe she should call her...maybe...

Screw it. She picked up the scissors that had been lying

next to her feet for half an hour and ran the sharp end down the middle of the box, slicing the packing tape and releasing the seal that kept the package closed. Carefully placing the scissors on a shelf behind her, she took a breath and parted the cardboard flaps.

Oh, wow.

One at a time, she lifted the items out and arranged them on the floor in front of her, then set the box aside. Jessica must have been planning one hot date. Candles, condoms, Lick-Me Flavor Lube? She suppressed a smile. Raspberry wasn't her favorite flavor, but she wasn't sure she was supposed to be the one tasting it. Jeff would have a heart attack if he could see her right now.

Evan would—no. She wouldn't think about Evan. He would probably laugh at her. He'd pinned her with the good-girl image she couldn't seem to escape, and sadly, he had been right. She had no proof that he had anything to do with the web page, and she'd only snapped at him out of frustration over her inability to have sex like a normal person. The hateful way he'd looked at her that afternoon had felt a thousand times more horrible than kissing him in the back of her car. Maybe she picked the wrong battles.

Back to happier thoughts. Back to the subject at hand, or rather, *in* her hand—a large, flexible, hot pink vibrator that she recognized from her product descriptions. One of the more expensive models, supposedly it worked quite well. She'd be lucky if Jessica didn't disown her for taking it out of its packaging. But she didn't plan to use it or anything. She was just looking. Jess would understand.

The soft texture surprised and delighted her. Years ago, she'd pictured sex toys as intimidating things used by savage people with bizarre fetishes. Goody-two-shoes, indeed. Her views had changed when she'd moved out on her own, met her ultra-sexual, detail-sharing girlfriends, and discovered erotic books and the Internet.

But nothing had left her more curious and open to the idea than what had happened at her desk on Evan's birthday.

She wrapped her hand around it and closed her eyes. The silky material brushed her skin while she caressed it with her fingertips. Bringing it to her shoulder, she folded her arms around each other and grazed her responsive flesh with both her hands and the toy. She imagined Evan staring at her with his intense eyes, using his hands to draw the vibrator slowly across her skin as he said—

"You're too high."

Her eyelids flew open. Like something out of a dream, he leaned against the doorframe, looking just as he had the night they met. All denim and black...and attentively watching her make out with herself in the middle of her office.

He crossed the room in three steps, leaving her no time to be humiliated. Kneeling in front of her, he tipped her chin up and forced her to see his eyes, wide and dark with passion. "I thought I told you to let me know if you needed anything."

"I..." Bree forgot how to speak and hoped she wouldn't need to remember. What she wanted to do with Evan at that moment didn't require conversation.

He lowered her arms and removed the vibrator from her fingers. "You're too high," he repeated. "It goes down here."

Of course she'd worn a skirt to work that day. She still sat with her legs crossed and Evan bent so close to her, there wasn't any room to unfold them and get into a decent position. So she was helpless to stop him when he traced a path under the fabric and up the inside of her thigh, positioning the pink tip against her thin panties and the burning flesh beneath them.

Then he turned it on.

With a gasp much louder than she'd intended, she surged

forward, only to be intercepted by his broad, hard chest. He buried his free hand in her hair and nuzzled her face until she inched her mouth close enough for him to plunge his tongue inside.

"Evan," she pleaded between kisses. "I don't think we're supposed to mess with the products."

Her knees shook when he moved the vibrator in a tiny circle. "You bought everything in that box," he said in a low voice, trailing his lips along her jaw line. "You own this stuff. You can do whatever you want with it."

Him. She wanted to do *him.*

She struggled to preserve her logical thought process, but it vanished, along with her self-control, when he turned up the speed. The sensations rippling through her began to snowball, and she gripped his shoulders like a life jacket while she rode a wave of excitement that crested and engulfed her before she could blink.

Crying out, she arched into the source of the sweet pressure, pushing the device harder against her sex until the last jolt subsided. She rested her lips on his neck and plunged her hands into his hair. Wordlessly, he held her. She shivered and worked to slow her breathing, marveling all the while at the gentle stroke of his fingers on her back.

"It does have other capabilities," he murmured when they broke apart, "but I think you get the idea."

He set the box and the toy aside and tugged her legs out from beneath her, offering his hand. Shakily, she accepted it and stood up, her high heels bringing her to eye level with him.

"I'm sorry about what I said today," she whispered.

"Me too."

She stared at him, stunned by the raw lust in his gaze. This was the kind of moment she fantasized about daily, the kind she'd wished for all those nights when Jeff had rolled over and given her ten minutes of his time. She used to believe true passion was reserved for bold people like Jessica. But Evan's eyes reflected barely-contained desire for *her*, and she'd waited long enough for her turn.

Maybe it was selfish, but she needed a hot and crazy sex session so she could quit thinking she was the only person in the world who hadn't had one. In fact, the more she thought about that, the hotter she felt and the more she wanted to get this show on the road.

Her lips trembled, but with a deep breath and a firm reminder that she owed herself this pleasure, she kissed him. His mouth met hers without hesitation and his belt buckle skimmed her abdomen, stoking the fire that hadn't burned out after the first release and making her ache for another. She groaned softly when his tongue stroked her neck, and just as she moved to ask him to touch her again—this time without the vibrator—the backs of her knees hit something leathery. They had stumbled their way over to her desk chair.

"Sit down, Bree."

The gentle command sent white-hot tremors down her spine. She did as he asked and he knelt in front of her once more, looking into her eyes while he reached for the buttons on her top. She drank in the sight of him, intoxicating as any drug—his silky dark hair, the rough hands making their way down her torso, the silver ring that added a hint of mischief to his blazing eyes. A thrill shot through her.

He released the last button and ran his fingers up the center of the shirt before pushing it aside. She sucked in a breath when the brisk air and his heated gaze swept over her breasts.

"You're beautiful." He moved his thumbs over her lace-covered nipples, and she could hardly see straight as he settled between her knees and dropped searing kisses on her neck, her chest, her stomach. He massaged her thighs while his tongue traced the top of her skirt, and only then did she figure out where he was going.

"Evan—"

"It's all right. I'll be nice." He nudged the hem of her skirt up and slipped a finger around the edge of her panties. She grew restless, yearning to give him full access to her body and at the same time, wanting to end the madness. Caught between fear and euphoria like a kid who'd outgrown her training wheels, she shifted in the chair and prepared to move away from his touch, but he stilled her with one slow, smooth stroke.

And then another.

Her head sagged against the back of the chair, and every last breath in her lungs departed. His caress teased her flesh like the brush of a thousand feathers, an exquisite reminder of the reason she'd decided to go through with this. It was too delicious to pass up.

Two minutes ago she'd been primed to tell him that no one had kissed her there before, but the last thing she wanted to do was scare him off with news about her oral virginity when he seemed ready to alleviate that problem. Just thinking about it must have made her moan, because she heard a strangled sound escape her throat and glanced down to see him watching her with warmth she hadn't imagined him to possess.

Evan smiled at her, then rose from his position on the floor and took a long look at her open shirt, the skirt hoisted to her waist, and the way her eyes kept shifting to the door as though someone would walk in any minute. "Would it make you feel better if I closed it?"

She nodded, eyelashes fluttering. Her nervousness came as no surprise to him. He knew her sex kitten persona was part of the job, an image she crafted with the same care as her provocative wardrobe and the company's marketing campaigns. But her inner seductress had the potential to match the one she displayed to the world, and he'd do his best to entice her to come out and play.

He wished he wouldn't have changed out of his work clothes before heading back to put in a few more hours at the office. His preppy dress pants allowed much more room for a raging hard-on. He'd nearly lost his mind right there in the doorway when he'd stumbled in and caught Bree seconds away from performing every man's dream. She had looked so tempting, so erotic, so...like someone who did not need to be giving *herself* an orgasm. The bruised ego she'd bestowed on him a few days earlier had puffed right back up when she'd come so easily in the palm of his hand.

As if that weren't enough to make him horny as hell, when he'd dared to dip his thumb beneath those black lace panties—and damn if he wasn't shocked when she let him—he'd found her hot, swollen, and ready to take every inch of him inside her.

Later. First, he needed to prove that his lovemaking skills went beyond the wham-bam she believed to be his norm.

He latched the door with a quiet click, then crossed the room and picked up the box of toys lying at Bree's feet. She sat forward in the chair and watched him arrange the items on her desk. He removed the lids from two candles and lit the wicks with some matches from a nearby drawer.

Carefully inspecting the rainbow of condom packets, he gave her an amused grin. "Looks like these are meant to act as dessert more than protection. Good thing I have my own."

Her mouth opened, her expression one of pure fascination. He felt a genuine urge to laugh—happily, not as a form of ridicule—something he hadn't experienced in a while. He didn't consider himself a person someone else could *need*, but right then, Bree looked like she needed him to push her body to an extent of physical pleasure she'd never known.

He could handle that.

He slid his arms around her middle and pulled her from the chair so she stood in front of him. "Does it turn you on to think about using one of those with me?"

Her lips barely moved in response, so he covered them with his own, his rigid cock searching for a way out of his zipper.

In due time.

He reveled in her feminine gasp as he wrapped his tongue around hers and pushed the straps of her top over her shoulders until the whole thing fell to the floor. One tug of the skirt from her hips and it joined the crumpled heap forming below them. She threw her head back. He chose a delicate spot behind her ear to suck on, leaving her skin pink and marking her as his.

When he'd discarded her bra, he stepped back and admired the sight of the flawless woman in front of him, her tight body clad only by a thong and high-heeled sandals with straps that reached halfway up her calves. Releasing a tension-filled breath, he grabbed her around the waist and drew her down to the floor.

She let out a little shriek, but when she settled on her back and he knelt above her, her eyes were huge with anticipation. She kept glancing at a point above his head, and he couldn't figure out what so captivated her until she bit her lower lip and gave him a naughty smile.

The ring in his brow. She liked it.

"You faker," he teased, reaching for one of the candles on top of her desk and snuffing out the flame. "All the trouble you give me about that thing, and it makes you hot."

She smiled and looked one more time at the small silver hoop. "Stop making me like you."

"Ah." He touched the wax to test its temperature. "Now she likes me."

"You're okay when you're not being a pain in my ass."

Now that was the Bree he knew. "Sweetheart, I plan to be a pain in places other than your ass."

She rewarded his statement with the astonished look he fully expected. Trying not to smile, he positioned the candle over one perfect breast.

"Don't worry," he said when she flinched. "This is PPH wax. It's meant to be played with. It won't burn you."

He turned the tin on its side, and a few drops of wax filtered out. He caught them with his finger and spread the smooth heat over her skin. Her back arched.

"Mmm," he groaned. "You like?"

Bree liked. She *loved*. Even while she lay on the floor of her office, almost naked with Evan on top of her, she couldn't believe any of it. He couldn't accuse her of being a prude after tonight.

Rubbing one of her peaked nipples with the wax, he cupped her other breast and laved the tip as he spoke to her. "You have the most amazing body."

"Please," she begged, unable to take any more of his teasing. She bunched his shirt in her hands and pulled it out of his jeans. "I want you naked with me. Now."

He allowed her to tug the shirt off but took her hand as it headed for the button of his pants. "No, ma'am. I'm not finished with you yet."

"But—"

Her protest faltered when he drew his palms down her legs and nudged them apart, leaving her wide open in front of him with only a scrap of wet lace to hide behind. And even that comfort disappeared when he pushed it aside to press a deep kiss on her intimate, exposed flesh. She shouted, and her hips rocked toward the source of the intense pleasure.

"Yes," his deep voice rumbled. "Scream my name. Tell me

you want me."

"I want you. Oh, God, I want you." She couldn't deny it. She couldn't fight it. She wanted him inside her—but she wouldn't argue if he insisted on finishing with her first.

The gentle strokes of his tongue made her shake with the need to climax. She gasped for breath and gave up on trying to be quiet when he applied hard pressure to that incessant tingling, massaging his mouth over her until the buzzing sensations filling her body gathered in that one tiny spot and shattered.

He shed the rest of his clothing in no time. She was still recovering from the spasm that had just rocked her entire body when he removed her sodden thong and eased into her. His length stretched and filled her, blurring her awareness of the outside world and connecting their bodies completely.

She relished the sensation, dizzy with rapture as each thrust relieved the heavy ache that had presented itself every time she'd thought of him since their encounter in the airport. Opening her eyes, to her surprise she found him looking right at her.

"Not what you remember, am I?" His voice swayed while he moved inside her. She shook her head, mesmerized by his raw stare, stunned by the tender way he was making love to her. She realized then that she'd been so caught up in what he was doing to her, she hadn't tried out any of the things she'd dreamed of doing to him.

Next time, she promised herself as he let out a soft curse and found his release. She wrapped her arms around his neck and held him close to her. Unless she managed to yank herself back to reality sometime very soon, there would definitely be a next time.

Chapter Eight

Distant thumping woke Bree from a deep slumber. She opened one eye and scanned the fuzzy shapes that made up her bedroom when she wasn't wearing her contacts. Rolling to her back, she sprawled on the bed and snuggled the blankets around her neck. Sunlight streamed through the window blinds, and every muscle in her body resisted movement. The morning had all the makings of a lazy Saturday. She considered closing her eyes and going right back to sleep, but an odd feeling nagged at her, warned her something was out of place...

Tuesday!

It may have been Saturday morning in her dreams, but reality's calendar read Tuesday, and she should have been at work an hour ago.

She leapt from her bed and dashed into the bathroom to turn on the shower. Why hadn't her alarm gone off? Why hadn't Todd called to find out where she was? Hopefully she would stay in Paula's good graces despite being late without an excuse. She usually arrived fifteen minutes before the workday began, and she never played hooky. She missed work only for emergencies, and oversleeping because she stayed up too late having sex didn't quite rank as an emergency.

Having sex?

Oh. God.

She'd slept with Evan last night.

So that explained her matted hair, the circles beneath her eyes, her aching body...and the Saturday-morning feeling of freedom that had greeted her when she'd awakened. Could anything compare to great sex followed by an entire day available to do nothing but reminisce about it? Still, despite the full day's work ahead of her and the nightmare she saw in the mirror, she couldn't feel too bad considering she'd just had the best sex of her life.

That couldn't be right. How could she have experienced such a thing with *Evan?* Maybe she had taken one too many ibuprofen pills while trying to annihilate a headache yesterday. She stepped into the shower and hurried through her morning routine, all the while pondering the insanity of the previous night.

Okay. Technically, it was the best sex of her life. How many orgasms did she have? Three—four? She'd lost count. That man knew how to touch her, and she couldn't for the life of her figure out how it had gone so wrong the first time. Her appetite for adventure had certainly been sated, but what about her integrity? Getting down and dirty in her office with a guy she barely knew wouldn't make any list of respectable actions.

But then, she didn't particularly want to be respectable anymore.

A dollop of hair gel and a bold layer of makeup helped her resemble less of a "before" photo and more of the sex goddess she presented to her coworkers on a daily basis. In the interest of comfort and regaining some inkling of modesty in front of Evan, she chose to wear a simple pair of low-rise pants, flats, and a comfy, fitted top. Her tired limbs balked at the idea of squeezing into another minidress or teetering around on four-inch heels.

In the mad rush out of her apartment, she almost tripped over a package lying outside the front door. The delivery guy's knocks must have woken her up earlier. Good thing, too, or she'd still be lolling around in bed while Paula signed her firing papers.

She tucked the box under her arm and took off down the stairs toward her car. She managed to make it to work by nine-thirty.

Paula had never come in before ten, and the sight of her in her office already would have made Bree crazy with worry over her tardiness—if not for the presence of two police officers who were probably not discussing her contract.

Trying not to stare, she crept past Paula's window and hurried to her desk, where she picked up the phone and buzzed Todd.

"Can I talk to you for a sec?" she asked urgently.

"Be right there."

When he popped his head in the doorway, Bree motioned for him to come in. "What on earth is going on? What's with the police?"

Todd sighed and sat down. "I'm not sure, but they've been in there interviewing Evan for half an hour."

Her heart skipped a beat. She hadn't seen Evan in the huddle around Paula's desk, but she'd been so shocked to see police, she had ducked away pretty fast.

"Why? What did he do?"

Todd leaned forward, his voice low. "I heard this from Lacy, so take it with a grain of salt. But she swears Paula mentioned theft to one of the officers, and apparently Evan has a record a mile long."

She swallowed, a useless action since the lump in her throat had grown too large to be forced back. The man she'd trusted with her body—and a lot more of her soul than she cared to think about—had a criminal record?

"That doesn't make sense," she said, mainly to make herself feel better. "Paula wouldn't have hired him if he were a danger to the company."

"Maybe she just took him in because he needed somewhere to go."

She frowned. "What do you mean? He's a marketing consultant. He's not exactly homeless." She would know. A few months ago, she'd seen his apartment with her own eyes, and it didn't resemble economy housing.

Todd crossed his arms. "I don't trust him. He was pretty shifty when I told him about the website, and Paula said he was a troublemaker when he was younger. Time doesn't change everything."

They talked for a few more minutes, and after Todd left, Bree felt sick. Was Evan using her to get access to something in the office? It was clear the two men didn't get along, but Todd and Paula had been friends for a long time, and she was certain he'd told her the truth about Evan's past. She could believe it too, given the bravado he'd shown her until last night.

She didn't know how she would face him. Now she had to wonder about his record, as if thoughts of last night weren't distracting enough. Her cheeks warmed. She tried to concentrate on reading her email, but her gaze shifted to the floor where the two of them had been naked and panting. He'd undressed her in that very *chair*. Her thighs tensed at the delicious memory.

Her dormant libido had never exercised so much control over her. Calm, careful Bree had gotten laid in her place of employment. Pride and exhilaration coursed through her at the way she'd solidified her new sexy side, and she ached for a repeat performance.

But that was out of the question. She'd given him the benefit of the doubt when it came to his pierced eyebrow and aversion to long-term relationships, but a criminal past was another story. Even if he hadn't done anything wrong at the office, he'd obviously done something before. Now that she'd experienced her sexual thrills—there were only a couple of things left on the list—it was time to focus on the future again. And in the long-term, Evan was completely wrong for her.

Todd had left her door open when he left, and out in the hall she saw Paula shake hands with the officers who then headed for the exit. When she heard the double doors close, she ran her hands through her hair to correct any wind damage that might have occurred on her way inside, then gathered her professionalism and set off to find Evan. If they could get their joint work done as soon as possible, she could avoid him for the rest of the day.

When she poked her head into his office, he was typing away at his computer, his expression so neutral she wondered if she'd hallucinated the authorities who had been there just moments ago. How could he change his looks so drastically yet melt her resolve like warm butter no matter which persona he chose? The seductive, intriguing rebel hid behind the intellectual consultant once more, but Bree found his business-casual getup as irresistible as those faded jeans he wore, the ones that cradled his tight ass and sizable—

"I didn't think you'd make it in today." His fingers paused above the keys when he saw her standing there.

"Why's that?"

The corner of his mouth turned up with its usual swagger. He shrugged. "I don't know. Playing hooky? Tired?"

"I don't play hooky. My alarm didn't go off." She raked her fingers through her hair again, determined to ignore the many ways he had pleased her. Deception was an offense she didn't take lightly, and there was a real possibility he'd fed her a pile of it.

"Don't worry, I told everyone you were sick so your flawless record wouldn't be tarnished."

She narrowed her eyes at his chuckling. "What's so funny?"

"You and your schizophrenic tendencies. People were running around like headless chickens when you didn't show up this morning. Seems you're never a minute late. Wouldn't they be shocked to know what their employee-of-the-month did on the floor of her office last night?"

He slid a purely sexual gaze over her body, clearly intending to let her know he remembered everything. She blushed, thought of his hands in her hair, his lips on her breast, his tongue...

His record.

She blinked. "They'd be happy to know it won't be happening again. Anyway, I just came to show you the brochure content I finished yesterday. It's in the folder called—"

"Is that a joke?" He stood, his expression changing from amusement to anger like he'd flipped a switch. "Is that how you do things? Once a man gets you off, you're finished with him?"

Her mouth opened in shock, but she managed to spout, "That's right," before she closed it, just to cut ties with him once and for all. She spun and retreated to her office, planning to stay there for the next eight hours so no one would see her bright red face. Her work would never get done if she couldn't say a word to Evan without picturing him naked above her. She needed a distraction, and fast. She could start a new marketing project, call Jessica...

Her package! She retrieved the delivery she'd stashed next to her bookshelf, ripped the tape open, and rifled through a sea of foam peanuts.

A teddy bear and a three-pack of bibs?

Great. The courier had left it at the wrong door and she'd ransacked her neighbor's baby gift. She studied the top flap of the box to find out which apartment she should return it to. *Jeffrey and Karla Warner, 1000 West Palm, Number 317.*

Delivery guy hadn't been half-asleep, then. Three-seventeen was Bree's place.

Jeffrey Warner was her ex-boyfriend.

He married her.

She stared at the names on the package, her heart racing. Jeff had gotten another woman pregnant and then married her before the baby's birth to avoid ruining his upstanding, medical-prodigy image. Nothing mattered to him more than his precious reputation. And according to the return address, his aunt Martha didn't get the news that he had moved out of West Palm about eight months ago.

She had spent three years with Jeff, lived with him for two, and he'd refused to consider getting married because he felt his demanding schedule would be detrimental to a family. Right. Now she knew the problem lay with her. He hadn't wanted her enough. He wanted Karla, whoever the hell that was. Bree had never met her and with any luck, she never would.

A monstrous hand clamped around her rib cage and squeezed. The pain of that day rushed back and she pushed her forehead into the top of her desk, cradling her hands over her hair. She'd had so many dreams of weddings and babies and fiftieth anniversaries.

She'd been so naive.

Drops of water fell from her eyes onto the box she still held in her lap. The wet circles formed slowly at first, then pelted into the cardboard like rain.

That's when she looked up and saw Evan.

"What's wrong?"

She quickly hid behind her arms again, but not before

Evan got a good look at the red splotches on her face. "Bree?"

"Nothing," came her muffled response. "Go away."

He closed her door, rolling his eyes. He'd been interrogated by the cops for no particular reason first thing this morning, and now his lover was blowing him off. What had he done to deserve this shitty day?

"Nothing my ass. What's going on?" He approached her chair and spotted a package in her lap. "Another one? What's the matter, this one wasn't as fun?"

She moved her head from side to side. Her shoulders shook. When he considered that she might regret what happened between them, he felt like he'd swallowed a brick. If sex with him had been so awful a second time, he might forget this whole run-his-own-business thing and start looking into careers at the monastery.

He put his hand on her back and she jumped a mile. "Hey, I'm just trying to help."

Finally, she lowered her arms. That casual outfit she wore softened the edge she typically created with spiky heels and tight clothes, but those big, moist eyes gave her away. She looked like a different person, much like the innocent girl he'd imagined after their first night together. But he wanted her as much as he'd wanted the siren in the black thong last night.

Something in her face changed as she looked at him. She put the box on her desk and rose from her chair. "Evan—"

"What is that?" He reached past her and pushed back the open flaps.

"No, don't..."

Baby stuff? He couldn't help glancing at her stomach, though he'd seen enough of it to know she couldn't possibly be pregnant. "Bree, you're not—"

"It's not mine." Grabbing the box out of his hands, she re-stuck the packing tape as best as she could, then pointed her fingernail at the label and glared at him. "It's not mine," she whispered again, stalking across the room to mess with the leaves on a fake tree.

Evan scanned the name and address. Jeffrey and Karla Warner? He turned to watch Bree, who stood with her back to him and her face in her hands.

My ex-boyfriend is expecting a baby any day now. Jeffrey. Jeff.

The sight of a woman he'd very recently made love to sobbing over the loss of her ex felt like a punch in the gut, but he ignored the feeling. Their night together had been purely physical, nothing that came close to whatever special thing she'd shared with Jeff.

He put the box down and joined her in front of the ficus. "Bree, I'm sorry."

She spun and grabbed his arms, throwing them around her waist while she pressed her mouth to his. He made a sound of surprise but held her tight, the heat of her aggression turning him on. She reached up to entwine her fingers in his hair. He stroked his tongue against her lips, his hands roaming down her back and squeezing the soft flesh of her ass.

His shaft stood at attention in his khakis. *She's rebounding,* he tried to convince it. *She's re—*

"Here," she said breathlessly, dragging them both to an extra chair in the corner of her office. She pressed her hands to the front of his chest and pushed him to a sitting position, then bent down and reached for the button of his pants.

"What...?"

"Shh." She fumbled with his zipper, and before he could stop her, she had his pants and boxers open and her lips wrapped around his cock.

"Shit—Bree, what are you—"

She gave him a hard suck and he dropped his head to the back of the chair. Not good. This was not good.

You cannot have sex with a woman while she's crying over her ex.

She moved up and down with torturous fury, and it took every ounce of his control to keep from coming right in her mouth.

Okay, so you can, but you shouldn't.

"Stop!"

She lifted her head. "Fine. We'll just go straight to—"

"No." He stood and stepped around her, tucking himself back in and fastening his belt before he changed his mind. "Straight to nothing. This is crazy."

Wearing an expression of near-madness, she ravaged him again, kissing him with enough force to back him into the bookshelf. "It feels to me like someone disagrees with you."

She rubbed her hands against his erection, a conspicuous bulge certain to make him the laughingstock of the office if he didn't remove himself from her grip. With iron strength, he took her wrists and held her still. "The door's unlocked and I have a meeting with Paula in ten minutes. I don't think this is the best time."

Hurt filled her eyes. She nodded slowly, turning away from him. "I guess you're right."

She returned to her desk and pounded the box of baby goods with her fist, either an attempt to make the tape stick or a tantrum in response to her ex's new status as a father.

When she'd come into his office to ditch him after sex—again—Evan had started to believe she was like every other woman he'd met in a bar. She didn't seem to have anything nice to say to him unless she was hot under her panties, and her innocent side could have been an act. Maybe she was a tease.

But now, having seen her freak out and attack him because of a baby gift, he suspected she was quite the opposite.

He spoke gently. "Is this Jeff guy the only person you've been with besides me?"

Bree scowled, but her eyes remained glued to her computer screen. "Of course not."

"You can tell me the truth. I'm not going to think less of you because you have standards, you know."

She looked at him, and for a moment it seemed like she might give in. But then she shook her head, her old aloofness stepping up to the plate. "Truth, huh? What's all this I'm hearing about your *record*?"

She spat the word like he shouldn't have dared to soil her with his dirty existence. That pissed him off, but at least it deflated what was left of the tent in his pants. He wondered how she had heard about the stunts he'd pulled as a kid, but that didn't even matter. Her reaction, judgmental as ever, did.

"So, that's what this is about." He crossed his arms. "You don't want to see me anymore because I have a 'record'. Guess what? I had a record yesterday, but you still thought I was good enough to sleep with."

"I guess that makes me zero for two."

Michelle knocked on the door jamb, temporarily numbing the prick of Bree's words. "Emergency staff meeting in five."

Evan turned just in time to see her black hair disappear around the corner. He'd explained away his disinterest with a vague discussion about not wanting to mix work and relationships. She'd insisted that she understood but had since avoided him like the plague. She probably saw right through his lame excuse.

Admittedly, he didn't follow the same logic when it came to Bree.

An emergency meeting could only mean bad news, and he had no idea what it was about. He needed to quit thinking with his dick and start doing his job, or he could kiss the CEO position goodbye. His preoccupation with Bree had muddied his priorities. So what if she wanted to have sex and walk away? That wasn't exactly a deal-breaker in regards to his future. Unemployment and the loss of dreams he'd worked toward since Tony died, well, that had the potential to send him back to the financial disaster from whence he came.

Not an option.

He moved to the conference room and took a seat across the table from Bree, taking care to look the other way so he wouldn't see her beautiful face or the condescending look in her eyes. Paula came in wearing a black blazer and skirt, a conservative look for his neon-and-lace sister. She also wore an angry frown.

"All right, I hate to bring everybody down, but we have a serious problem."

Everyone listened. Paula paced, cell phone in hand. "There's been a theft in the office. I'm expecting a call back from the police department regarding any suspicious activities that have taken place recently, but the officers I spoke with don't know of too many incidents in this area. They suggested it might be an inside job."

She paused. Evan's heart sank, his impromptu meeting with police no longer a mystery. He'd done his share of stealing as a teenager who had possessed few material things and even less common sense.

But Paula wasn't finished. "I'm inclined to believe him."

Several staff members gasped. Everybody started talking at once. She held up her hands. "People, please. Since we're all here, I need you to listen up."

"What was stolen?" someone called out.

"We're missing an entire box of Bath Buddies that just came in last week. Also some other inventory, some petty cash...a bunch of things. Now, if this is an inside job and the culprit turns himself or herself in by the end of the day, I won't press charges. But you can expect to return the property or pay for it, and find employment elsewhere."

Lacy took in Paula's every word with wide eyes. She probably couldn't wait to start spreading rumors and hyping suspects. "When was it taken?" she asked, almost excitedly.

Paula glanced at each and every one of them in turn before answering.

"Last night."

Chapter Nine

The last time Michelle felt this sick, she'd been eighteen and staring into a toilet while a bottle of cheap whiskey came back up.

She hated causing trouble for the company. Paula had shown her nothing but kindness since her first day, but there'd be worse hell to pay than petty theft if she didn't resolve her issues with a certain colleague. With any luck, the havoc in her stomach this time would result in something better than getting slapped with a DUI and losing two days' worth of wages to a hangover.

"Hey, girlie. Wanna have lunch?"

She glanced up from mounds of paperwork to see Lacy on the other side of her desk, a steaming plate of Indian food in her hand. Just the smell of all that curry made Michelle's stomach ache for a source of fuel more substantial than the Pop-Tart she'd eaten five hours ago.

"I wish I had time, but this theft stuff is making my job a nightmare." She wondered if Harry had anticipated *that* when he'd devised his great plan. Not that he gave a damn about her comfort or convenience.

Eyes wide, Lacy pulled up a chair and placed the plate on her lap. "You know, everyone thinks Bree is behind this," she whispered between forkfuls of rice.

Michelle pulled a granola bar from her drawer and peeled off the wrapper, doing her best to keep her voice even. "That's odd. What about the guys? Evan's new here and Todd seems to be working late a lot." Which was why she always made sure to get the hell out by five o'clock.

Lacy shook her head. "They're too close to Paula. I heard her explaining to the cops that there's no way Evan could be involved. Anyway, Bree does the most work with the website and the Bath Buddies. It just makes sense."

Wonderful. It may have made sense, but it didn't do her a lick of good. She choked down the rest of her peanut butter and honey bar, which suddenly tasted like dog food.

"And get this," Lacy continued. "Paula didn't want to leak all the details in the meeting, but supposedly we're missing a *lot* more money than 'petty cash'. That's why she called the police!"

By the time Lacy finished the sentence, she was squealing more than a newly crowned prom queen. She really got off on spreading rumors. Michelle raised a brow.

"Where do you hear all this stuff?"

"Around. Todd told me about the money."

The foul wave that washed through her had the makings of morning sickness, food poisoning *and* a nasty hangover in one tidy combination. If Paula trusted Todd with details of the investigation, and Evan was her brother, then the list of possible suspects was dwindling fast. Only a few people in the office had access to the website and administrative business. At the top of the list would be Bree...and *her.*

Her fists clenched. If Harry didn't manage to frame the right person, she'd dump him from her life for good. She wasn't kissing his ass just to mess up more than she had in the first place.

The phone rang. Lacy stood, indicating she'd be back later. Michelle waved and picked up the receiver. "Paula's Pleasure

House, may I help you?"

"I don't think you have a choice."

She sighed. "Damn it, Harry, I told you not to call me here." Someone had invented cell phones for a reason—namely so she didn't get busted if the cops decided to tap the business line.

"Just checking in on my protégé. How's the job going?"

"Busy. I need to get off the phone and work."

"I wasn't talking about that job."

She gritted her teeth, beginning to regret that she'd ever asked for his help. "I don't know why you're asking me, because according to what I just heard, a hell of a lot more was stolen than I ever touched."

His laugh chilled her to the bone. "Sorry about that, babe. But really, taking some shit off a web page? Filching a bunch of dildos? You're an amateur. Hacking into a bank account, now that's talent. I had to up the stakes a bit to make this work."

"It's *not* working. Todd isn't even a suspect, and your stupid plan is moot if he doesn't become one."

"I'll handle that. You just think about where you want to hook up with me, babe. I just won enough dough to get us a real nice room downtown."

She heard him clicking away at his keyboard, undoubtedly in the middle of another poker game. Her stomach turned. "You're disgusting. Quit calling me 'babe'."

"Whatever you say, sweetheart. Don't you worry. This will all be over by next week."

Bree kicked off her high-heeled pumps and heard them clunk against the back of her desk. Two days ago, she'd worn something comfortable and set off a disastrous chain of events—PPH had been robbed, Jeff had gotten married and she had made a complete idiot of herself in front of Evan. She took that as a sign she would do well to stop being lazy about keeping up her image.

So now she sat rigidly in her chair, sucking in any imperfections and pretending she could breathe in the electric blue scoop-neck dress she'd borrowed from Jessica. Though it barely covered her butt, she couldn't be concerned with modesty anymore. She had to put every effort into burying the vulnerabilities she'd carelessly let out into the open since making love with Evan.

She had wanted adventure, a sexual interlude that would take her from nice to naughty and provide valuable experience for her personal and professional lives. He had provided that in the best possible way. But she hadn't planned to sob all over him about the most emotionally painful event of her life—their relationship was physical, not personal.

Man alive, was it physical. She couldn't stop thinking about the intoxicating taste of him, the thrill of having had him in her mouth. Never in her life had she believed she would enjoy that kind of thing, yet in that moment, she found herself wanting to lave him until he begged her to stop.

Which, essentially, he did. But not the way she wanted him to. In fact, he'd called her bluff and guessed the lackluster truth—he was the second partner she'd ever had. Her attempts to convince him of her sensual nature were not going well, and she only had a few days left before she would meet with Paula about her contract.

"We're going to lunch."

Evan beckoned from her doorway, and her gaze fell below his belt. Her face warm, she tried to focus on his features, but she found that view equally enticing.

"I'm sorry, what?"

"We're going to lunch," he repeated. Without cracking a smile, he entered her office, snatched her purse from the floor and held it out to her.

"Aren't you a charmer with the ladies?"

"We have to talk about the theft. Alone."

Did she look as green as she felt? The nausea rising in her chest stemmed from either the knowledge that she and Evan had been the only ones in the office that night and therefore were the sole suspects—or the thought that someone could have listened to the sex soundtrack playing behind her closed door.

She was sure she'd screamed at least once and moaned a bunch before that. The idea of her coworkers knowing she'd had sex in her office—with the marketing consultant, no less— would be almost as humiliating as being fired for a crime she didn't commit.

Sighing, she took her bag and followed him. If Evan doubted her innocence, that was fine. She felt the same way about him, and this would be the perfect chance to find out if he had anything to do with vandalizing the site as well as set him straight on the fact that she was no thief.

They drove—in separate cars, to avoid becoming the subject of Lacy's relentless gossip—to a local deli, where Bree picked at a chicken salad, and Evan stared at her between bites of a roast beef sandwich.

Finally, he wiped his hands on a napkin and wadded it up, then pointed it at her. "I need to know if you're involved in this."

She pretended to look frightened. "Or you'll strike me with that bacteria-laden napkin?"

"Not funny. Doesn't it matter to you that somebody is trying to hurt our business?"

"Of course it does. You'll have other clients, but PPH pays my bills. So quit looking at me like I'm on some kind of sabotage mission."

He studied his empty plate in silence. "I guess that makes sense."

"Yeah. Maybe you should be the one talking to *me* about what happened to the Bath Buddy page last week."

His head snapped up. "You know I didn't have anything to do with that."

"Do I?" She pushed her dish aside and leaned across the table. "You're the only other person who has access to the web files. I had just showed you where to find them, remember? Isn't that convenient?"

"Todd knows where the files are."

"Todd's been working with Paula since the company opened its doors. They're best friends. Give me a break."

"Look, none of that changes the fact that you and I were the only people in the office the night those things were stolen. What exactly would you make of that?"

She closed her eyes, envisioning Evan's awed expression when he had walked into her office and taken that vibrator from her. The gentle touch of his fingers that so strongly contradicted his tough-guy image. Her clothes, burning hot trails down her skin as he slipped them off her anticipative body.

Once again, she considered the possibility that someone might have witnessed their noisy affair. The quest to regain control over her emotions fell from importance in the face of the reality that as a temporary employee, she was the most disposable. If Paula suspected for even a moment that she had something to do with the trouble at work, or if word got around that she had a habit of sleeping with her colleagues, she'd be let go the minute her contract ended.

She couldn't let that happen. Her employment with PPH

was central to her newfound exotic lifestyle. She spent ten hours a day playing with—researching, actually—sex toys and composing prose meant to convince others they needed to play with them too. She couldn't exactly duplicate that kind of career at any other place in town. Where would she go if she lost her job?

Back to some cube-and-suit dungeon. Back to life as Miss Does-As-She's-Told, the dependable good girl who did everything right and ended up unhappy and alone. The girl who obeyed her parents the way she did when she was fourteen and wore a long-sleeved velvet dress to an outdoor party in the middle of July, because according to her mother, the tank dress showed too much skin and the pink T-shirt was too transparent. There were, after all, going to be *boys* at the event.

A shiver traveled down her spine.

Never. She would never go back to that.

She stared at Evan, her voice panicked. "You don't think anyone else could have been in there, do you?"

He shook his head. "Unlikely. Only employees have keys to the office, and we're located in the middle of a large building. I doubt a stranger would randomly choose to rob our suite."

Relief surged through her. "Right. Good."

His forehead crinkled. "Good? You know that leaves only you and me as suspects."

"No, good because..."

She couldn't finish her sentence. She could not talk to Evan about what they had done. Not when a single memory of it made her think about clearing the table, climbing on top of it, and asking him if he wanted dessert.

The twinkle returned to his eye, and she felt like jumping for joy. He'd been so serious, so bent on playing detective that she'd wondered if he even remembered their floor aerobics.

"I think we're safe, Bree. I have a feeling Paula would have kicked us both to the curb already if she knew what was going on in your office. She doesn't play around with her company."

"Even when her own brother is involved?"

"Especially when her own brother is involved."

She nodded and cleared her throat. "Well, then. Are you going to admit that you did it?"

"What?"

"Come on, Evan. You took the stuff. A joke on Paula, a prank on me...you have possible motives. And I would never—"

She stopped when she realized what she had almost said. She'd almost suggested that someone of her caliber, her high-society upbringing, would never stoop to stealing.

Sure enough, his gaze darkened. The man was perceptive as a mind-reader. "You would never steal."

"I wouldn't." She shifted her gaze to the table and prayed he wouldn't be insulted by her comment.

"But I would."

Damn.

"I didn't mean—"

"Let's go." He stood and marched to the trash bin, dumping the contents of his tray inside.

She followed, guilty as any convict. "Evan, please wait."

He opened the door and fixed her with the look her father used to give her when she said something rude in front of houseguests. She trudged in his direction, sure that if she had a tail it would be between her legs. Surprisingly, he did wait, and held the door for her. They walked to their cars in silence.

"Evan, I—"

He put a finger to his lips. She closed her mouth.

With a heavy sigh, he took her arms and drew her close to

him, speaking in a low tone. "Let me explain something to you. The *record* you're so worried about is, first of all, a juvenile one. Vandalizing cars and swiping junk food from convenience stores are the worst things on it."

She bit her lip. Not an ideal childhood, but at least he wasn't a felon.

"My 'pierced face', as you so kindly referred to it in the airport, isn't a symbol of rebellion," he continued. "It might have started out that way, but things changed."

She frowned. The distant spark in his eyes went beyond the hint of sarcasm and mischief she liked so much. In fact, he looked more than a little angry, though the sentiment didn't seem directed at her.

"What do you mean?" she asked, hoping he wouldn't choose that moment to show her an explosive temper.

He didn't. He just gazed into the sky, his brows pushed down with negative emotions. "My best friend Tony and I had it done at the same time when we were twenty. We went with a bunch of people to this dump in the middle of town one night. Everybody pierced something, and some of the guys got tattoos. I didn't, by the way. I just told you that to rile you up."

With a tiny smile, she chewed her lip again and looked at the ground. She deserved that.

"Anyway, we were walking back to the car when some kid came flying down the street in his daddy's sports car and ran right into Tony. Killed him on the spot."

Bree blinked, sure she hadn't heard him right.

But he was looking at her now, his expression filled with intense sadness and unquestionable honesty. She reached behind her and grappled for the handle of her car door, supporting herself against the window. Time seemed to stop while shock, sympathy, and guilt churned in her stomach.

"Oh, my God," was all she could say.

"The kid kept right on driving. Our crowd wasn't sober enough or fast enough to get the plate number, and since the cops saw Tony as a trashy street kid who'd been drinking too much, they didn't bother to spend much time investigating his case. He didn't have any family to protest that. I keep this as a reminder of him."

He touched the small ring in a gesture that resembled a salute. Her eyes burned. How could she have been so judgmental? Every negative label she'd placed on him had started with that blasted piece of jewelry, which all along had been a memento of his departed best friend.

She was a horrible person.

"I'm so sorry." Her hand went to her mouth. "I didn't—oh, I'm just so sorry."

He took her wrist and gently pulled it away from her face. "It's okay. You didn't know. I didn't tell you."

"It doesn't matter, I still—"

"Hey." He took her face in his hands and used his thumb to wipe a tear from her cheek. "It's okay."

With that, he kissed her, and she gasped his breath into her mouth. She ached to wrap her arms around him and give him an extended apology for her inexcusable narrow-mindedness, but he simply rested his lips on hers for a long moment, then pulled away and unlocked his car.

She was still watching in disbelief, trying to comprehend the story of his tragic past, when he looked up from his position in the driver's seat and hung his arm out the window to ask her a question she never thought she'd take seriously.

"Why don't you have a drink with me this weekend?"

And out of her mouth came the answer she never thought she'd give him.

"Sure."

Chapter Ten

Evan stifled a caveman-like urge to pound his chest and wondered if Bree could feel the eyes of every male in the room gawking at her. Stunningly draped in a red strapless dress that skimmed her luscious outline and ended just below her knees, she sat on the edge of a leather chair, her ankles crossed and the tips of her sandals grazing the floor.

Undoubtedly, the men saw a gorgeous picture of confidence and sophistication. He agreed with the latter assessment, but he caught the way she nervously twirled her martini and flicked those turquoise eyes back and forth between his own gaze and the crowd.

"This place is beautiful," she said, surveying the small, swank club. Located inside a luxury hotel, the place was done up almost entirely in black, from the shining floors to the cushy furniture and sleek bar. The way the red accent lighting matched that hot dress of hers nearly drove him crazy. He wanted her enough without the encouragement of the sexually charged atmosphere created by an establishment clearly targeted for the singles scene.

He smiled and took a swig of his vodka tonic. "It seems more your style than a place like Barry's."

She rolled her eyes. "Yeah, it's my 'style', but by the time I was old enough to drink I was sick of tiptoeing around the upscale world, so I've never actually been here before."

"I made a bad choice, then?"

"No, it's fine. I haven't been out anywhere nice in a while." She looked away as soon as the words left her mouth, making him wonder yet again which side of her—the sex goddess or the sweet angel—was the real Bree.

It was clear she meant she hadn't been on a date in a while, which he doubted she'd want to talk about, so he changed the subject. "So, if you hate rich people, why do you want to live like one?"

She gave him a questioning look.

"I get this feeling you live in an apartment that rents for more than a mortgage payment, pay three times what you should for clothes and date guys who wear suits to work every day. But you said you're sick of the upscale world."

A brief flash of shock crossed her features, but she pulled herself together quickly. "I do like some high-end things, I admit. I like being able to afford the things I want. I just can't stand the way people with money act so...perfect. So fake. 'Children should be seen, not heard.' You know."

He chuckled. "You've heard that one before, I'm guessing."

"My parents are like porcelain dolls. I'd rather not discuss them. What about you?"

"Me?"

"You and Paula. What's your family like?"

He took a long swallow of his drink to buy some time. He never divulged personal information to women—or anyone, for that matter—so why was he being so honest with Bree? He hadn't spoken about Tony in years until yesterday. Her accidental insult had irked him enough to tell her the truth, and he wanted to believe he'd only been trying to set her straight about his ethics—namely, that he had some—once and for all.

But the fact was, he wanted her to know him, and he wanted to know her. Now, while they had a chance to enjoy each other's company—and maybe even go for another romp in her office. Once Paula announced his imminent takeover of her position as CEO, his time with Bree would end. He'd become her boss, and anything more than a casual friendship would be out of the question.

Plus, she was bound to be furious when she found out his gig as PPH's marketing consultant had been a cover all along.

"Paula and I are the only kids, and my parents always treated us well. But we didn't have much money when I was growing up."

His chest tightened. If he had heard one story from his grandparents, he'd heard a thousand—tales of his mom and dad's younger days, when they had been a poster couple. Happy, in love, with a cushy bank account and a life filled with possibilities.

Then Paula came along, and their mother left her career to stay home. Money grew tight, but they got by. Five years later, Evan was born, his father lost his job and couldn't find another decent one. They spent the next several years scraping to feed their children until finally, when he was twelve, the stress of their financial disaster doused whatever fire they might have had and they divorced.

As far as he could tell, his parents would be living it up if they hadn't gotten married, hadn't had children, hadn't sacrificed paychecks for a bigger family that couldn't be happy under the circumstances. He'd grown up wearing twenty-five-cent garage sale clothes, playing with sticks and dirt in lieu of toys and listening to other kids chatter about birthday parties and holiday gifts he was too poor to experience.

He refused to live at the bottom of the barrel ever again, and he wouldn't conceive children to put *them* there, either. He had worked hard to climb out of poverty and had no plans to jump back in by marrying a woman who would expect him to take the next logical step and reproduce.

Which was why he spent his spare time in bars picking up strangers who wanted an hour of fun, instead of settling down with a nice girl he could introduce to his mother like the rest of his aging buddies had done.

"I was in the wrong crowd when I was a teenager because I didn't have much to do beyond hanging out on the street," he explained when Bree indicated she wanted to hear more. "But after Tony...well, we always swore at least one of us would go to college and make something of ourselves. So when he was gone, it was up to me. I got enough financial assistance to get a four-year degree, and someday I'm going to run my own business."

Guilt gnawed at him, urged him to come clean about the real reason Paula had hired him. But when Bree reached over and rested her hand on his leg, he only felt the swells of lust billowing through him.

"I don't doubt that for a minute," she said softly.

His body had warmed at her touch, but it damn near combusted when he saw the approval in her smile. What was wrong with him? He'd never given a second thought to anyone's opinion other than Paula and Tony. No one else had ever believed him capable of success.

But right then, Bree looked like she did.

He leaned across the tiny table and moved his lips against hers, brushing his thumbs over her cheeks. She wrapped her fingers around his wrists like she might stop him, but her kiss said otherwise. Only when he heard his glass tip over and opened his eyes did he notice her astonished stare.

He glanced at the ice cubes melting on the table, imagining how fast she'd go back to hating him if he turned her high-priced outfit into a sticky mess. "Oh, no. Did I spill this on you?"

She patted the front of her dress but didn't appear concerned about it. "No...it's just that Jeff never kissed me in public. He thought it was crude. We always had to be 'on' when we went out."

"On? What is that?"

"Poised. Prepared to run into a country club director at any given moment. Like flawless, expensive statues."

"He sounds like a jerk. Maybe it's good that he left."

"It wasn't just him. My parents expect the same thing. Everyone does, except my friends."

Her jaw clenched, and Evan knew an overwhelming need to take her in his arms, make love to her for hours and tell her how beautiful and perfect she was. So this was how she had lived most of her life—under constant scrutiny, hiding behind stiff manners and forbidden to explore her real desires.

This was why she worked at Paula's Pleasure House.

Suddenly he knew, without a doubt, she had nothing to do with the burglary.

The words slipped out without hesitation. "Come home with me."

She blinked. "Do what?"

If she agreed, it would carry their relationship beyond office doors. He understood the implications of that. He understood the danger.

He didn't care. He needed to hold her, needed to make her forget the people who didn't recognize her beauty, her creativity, her uniqueness.

"Come home with me. If you don't remember how to get there, you can follow me. Or leave your car here and I'll—"

"No." She took a deep breath that sounded as on-edge as he felt. "I'll drive."

"Déjà vu?"

At the same time Evan asked the quiet question, Bree felt his hands on her shoulders and relaxed into them. Why did she suddenly feel so comfortable with this man? And not only the man, but the place—the same living room where not so long ago, she had frantically called Jessica and begged for an escape plan.

"No," she answered. "Last time I just wanted to go home. This time there's nowhere I'd rather be."

He smiled before she kissed him, a deep, lingering kiss that underscored her intentions. Tonight, she wanted to make love with this magnificent man who continued to astound her with his warmth, kindness, and passion. She didn't even mind that she had confessed her not-so-wild past—clearly, it hadn't turned him off.

"I'd like to see your bed again," she whispered.

A low rumble sounded in the back of his throat. "Yes, ma'am."

He picked her up and carried her through the entrance to his room. She kicked off her shoes while her legs dangled over his elbow, then he let her down next to the bed with her back to him.

He unzipped her dress and it dropped to the floor, revealing another lacy thong and no bra, choices she'd made as she dressed earlier that evening with erotic thoughts of him bombarding her. She heard his breath catch when he tugged the tiny lingerie down to her ankles. She stepped out of it and faced him, releasing a soft moan as he slid a finger between her legs.

"Ah, ah," she chided him, guiding his hand away before she lost the will to do so. "It's my turn to play with you."

If she were with anyone else, the words would have made her blush. She'd lain in bed so many nights with Jeff, too timid to speak a word. She used to think it was her shyness that had caused their boring sex life. Now, though, she wondered if she'd just never been moved to say anything. Even Jeff's best lovemaking effort hadn't once made her feel as hot, sexy, and crazy with desire as Evan did every time he looked at her.

"I don't think I can argue with that," he said.

She unbuttoned his shirt and while he slipped it off, she stared in awe at his perfect pecs and washboard stomach. She opened her lips and tasted the beautiful tan color of his skin, entwined her fingers in the scant black hair on his chest. He smelled amazing, like a splash of musk, a single glass of alcohol and the faint beginnings of sweat. Like rough, sexual male.

He sank his hands into her hair as she bent down, knelt to the floor and took his pants and boxers down in one fell swoop. "Is now a good time?" she couldn't help asking.

She heard gentle laughter and gazed up to find him watching her with an amused little grin.

"Now works for me."

She braced one hand against his hip and wrapped the other around the firm, hot arousal eagerly reaching out to her. When she wet her lips and encircled the head of his cock, he gasped and rocked slightly forward, moving further into her mouth. She laved him, sucked on him, felt the thrill of his pleased groans pulse through her and settle at the junction of her thighs.

The harder he got, the more she needed to feel that part of him plunge into her. When she couldn't stand it anymore, she stood and kissed him with urgency.

"Please, Evan—"

"Hold on to the bed, sweetheart."

The way he called her sweetheart must have turned her mind to mush, because she couldn't have understood him right. Did he say—

"Turn around, baby. Like that."

She nearly fainted when she felt his naked body against her backside. She bunched the blanket in her fists as he filled her and made contact with something inside her that felt so good she cried out loud. He moved faster, drove harder until she shouted her delight with abandon and pushed back to meet his every thrust. She wanted to imprint her image in his mind so their short time together would be an experience he'd never forget.

Did she even possess the sexual skills to do something like that?

"Bree, I want you to come for me."

He snaked his hand around her hip and glided his fingers over her wet folds, stroking her clit until a charge strong as lightning propelled her over the edge. She gasped with pleasure and felt Evan clench behind her. He pushed into her one last time before wrapping his arms around her with a shudder.

Clearly, she didn't need to question *his* skills.

He released her and turned to dispose of the condom. When he returned to the bed, she stood holding her dress in front of her, either concealing her nudity or getting ready to leave.

Little did she know, neither of those were an option. He had every intention of spending more time tasting her body and exploring her mind.

A lot more time.

He took the gauzy fabric from her and laid it over his nightstand. "Did you think we were done already?"

Her floored expression said it all. "I guess so."

"Never had a man go more than once, huh?"

"Um...I...no." Her gaze shifted to the small container he held in his hand. "What's that?"

"Just a little something I picked up at work. Consider it my contribution to your paycheck."

He lifted his palm and she squinted to read the small print through the darkness. "Bawdy Body Paint."

Her eyes widened and she gave him the grin of a good girl being bad, the one he had seen the last time they'd made love. "Mmm, I can't pass up an opportunity to eat chocolate."

"I can't pass up an opportunity to eat *you*." He placed the jar on his bed and pulled her into a deep kiss that left them both breathless. Then he guided her down onto his sheets.

God, she was beautiful. That look of doe-eyed innocence turned him on even more than her sexy wardrobe. He'd seen mini-skirts and stilettos in nightclubs across the country, and sex with the ladies they belonged to had always been the same. Fast, rough, impersonal—the way he'd lived most of his life. It allowed him to stay distracted from his past and blindly move forward, enjoying all the fun he could finally afford to have. It kept him from getting close to anyone so he'd never have to consider things like marriage and babies.

He knew the tough image he created when he went socializing made him a good candidate for a one-night stand. Women looked at him and saw the same thing Bree did that first night—an attractive yet empty-headed punk. The perfect guy for purely physical, meaningless, thanks-and-nice-knowing-you sex. He preferred it that way, liked the fact that he could have a good time without getting bogged down in relationship mumbo-jumbo that would eventually have him working three jobs to put food on the table.

But this—showing Bree how satisfying sex could be with a little creativity, watching her reactions, feeling her touch him and respond to him as though he held the key to some magical world she'd otherwise never have access to—it felt even better. Invigorating.

Special.

And highly erotic. Those dilated turquoise eyes watched his every move while he twisted the lid off the jar of body paint. Her chest rose and fell with heavy breaths, and she trembled though he kept the thermostat in his apartment at a comfortable level.

He dipped a small brush into the chocolate and crouched over her on the mattress. "So," he said into her ear, "where should I take my first bite?"

Her eyelids dropped closed. With a stifled moan, she grabbed his free hand and moved it to her right breast. His shaft tightened with one look at that peaked, rose-colored nipple.

He grazed a bit of syrup over it. "You're right," he told her. "That looks good." And he licked her clean.

Her gasp could have sucked all the oxygen out of the room. Her fingernails dug into his back as he repeated the process with the other nipple before pulling back and looking into her stunned and aroused face. "Good?"

"Good," she puffed.

With a pleased smile, he planted tiny kisses all over her stomach, then retrieved his brush and sat back. With slow, tantalizing strokes, he drew a smiley face across her abdomen, using her navel as the nose.

She lifted her head to inspect his handiwork. "I don't like it," she said, though he doubted the truth of that statement given her wide grin. "Clean it off right now."

"My, my, she's a bossy one."

She laughed. "Damn right."

"Well, then. As you wish, mistress." He leaned down and lapped up the chocolate. Her hips rose when his mouth touched the places so close to her sex.

"Let me have that," she said, pulling his attention from the spot between her legs he longed to kiss.

He twirled the brush between his fingers. "You mean this?"

She plucked it from his hand, and he watched her smooth the bristles through the rich sauce. The more time they spent together, the more aggressive she became, and he liked it. A lot. Conveniently, he was kneeling in front of her, and she neatly painted his cock, her sexy eyes never leaving his.

His rent payment. The dentist. His gaze shot to the ceiling as he thought of something, anything to keep from exploding right there in her face.

She chose that moment to eat her chocolate creation.

The suction of her mouth was nearly the end of him. He grabbed her hair and she looked up, her lips swollen with her efforts to please him. "No," he choked. "No more."

Setting the jar and brush aside, he donned another condom and pressed her back against the bed. "Oh, yes," she breathed against his neck.

"Do you want me?"

"*Yes.*"

Desire rolled like thunder in his throat while he moved inside her. They were joined, but he wanted more. He wanted to sink into her warm, welcoming body as deeply as he could. Gently, he positioned her leg over his shoulder. When she didn't argue, he eased back and then plunged into her.

Her moan permeated both the room and the barricade that usually blocked off his emotions. It wasn't that fabricated, porn-star yelp he was used to hearing, but an involuntary release of pleasure that came not because she had a dick inside her, but because she had *him* inside her. He could feel it. He could tell by the fierce way she held onto him and by the captivated look in her eyes.

In that moment, he knew the difference between having sex and making love.

"Bree, is this okay?"

"Yes." She closed her eyes again, her breathing ragged as she arched her body to meet his rhythmic movements. "I have to tell you something. You were right. You're only the second."

"That's okay, sweetie." The words came out in a rush of air. He thrust harder, devouring her cries with long kisses, the significance of her confession running through his mind. Just as he reached the brink of orgasm, she nodded her head and shivered, and they shared a quaking climax that far surpassed any sexual experience he'd ever had.

Yet while he held her trembling body in his arms, he feared he had just gotten dangerously, irreversibly close to someone.

Chapter Eleven

The apartment that had scared Bree half to death a few months ago was actually quite cozy. Her toes sank into the taupe carpet, and dim lamps warmed every corner. A flat-screen television and large sofa were the only furnishings in the modest living room.

It reminded her of her own place—clean, open, uncluttered. The only difference lay in the motorcycle décor that adorned the walls and shelves, while she collected dog trinkets and pretty vases.

"You want a bike?" she asked Evan when he joined her on the sofa and offered her a cup of steaming coffee. She took it carefully, wrapping her palms around the soothing warmth of the mug.

He looked around at the various posters and gave her a boyish grin. "Yeah, when I can afford it. There's fun and freedom in those things a car can't provide."

She didn't doubt it. That sounded like something Evan would want. Fun and freedom, in his choice of transportation and his relationships. Another reason she'd do well to keep her emotions out of this fling and remember that she was sleeping with him purely for novelty, a fact she had forgotten when they were drowning in each other's eyes in his bedroom.

"Why haven't you dated anyone since your ex knocked up another woman?"

She pulled the mug back from her lips at the abrupt change in subject. "I, um, just haven't been able to find the right guy. My parents won't even attend my wedding, much less pay for it, unless the groom is practically identical to Jeff."

Evan's eyes narrowed. "You can't tell me they approve of a man cheating on you like that."

A sinking feeling settled in her stomach as she realized he was about to pry into her past—and she was going to let him.

"They don't know."

"They don't know what? How he treated you? Don't they know about the baby?"

"No. I told them Jeff and I weren't getting along so I broke things off. They don't know what he did."

"You'd rather be alone at your wedding than tell them the truth?"

"You don't understand. Jeff is very well-respected in my family's social circle. They'd never believe me, and you can damn well bet he wouldn't be honest about it." She swallowed, the rich aroma of the coffee absorbed by the pungent taste of disappointment. "They also don't know about my employment with Paula. They still think I have a 'respectable' job with a software company."

He stared at her for so long and in such silence, she took another sip from her mug for a distraction. She often questioned the erratic state of her family life, but Evan's appalled expression made obvious how troubled it was.

"Let me get this straight." He set his half-empty cup on the floor and crossed his ankle over his knee. "You haven't told your parents the truth about your breakup or your job? You're living a lie."

Well, that sounded a little harsh, didn't it?

"No, I'm not," she insisted. "I'm just avoiding an unpleasant confrontation that would probably lead to complete alienation from my parents, relatives and the general crowd I grew up with. It sucks, I know, but it's what I was born into and I can't cut myself off from everything—"

She stopped as the truth dawned on her. When she'd accepted the job at Paula's Pleasure House, her intention *had* been to cut herself off from everything she knew. To erase the sober, passionless life that had culminated in nothing but heartbreak. To become someone else...or at least pretend to be someone else. It was the reason she'd approached Evan at the club that first night—it was the reason she continued to spend time in his bed.

Except their recent interactions seemed to suggest he was more than a plaything to her. Hot sex and tossed-off wisecracks were safe, impersonal, and good practice for her new outrageous personality. And that was what they had...before.

But all this—the chivalrous date, the extended lovemaking, the intimate conversation—this bordered on tender. It wasn't rebellious or meaningless or the pure sexual fun she'd set out to have. Their fling suddenly had all the makings of a relationship, one that could easily lead to the same trap of attachment and heartbreak she'd fallen into before.

She jumped up from the couch and walked her unfinished coffee to the sink, then stepped into her shoes and looked around for her purse. If she stayed one more minute, she'd suffocate. Or worse, she'd fall for him.

He stood and headed toward her. "What are you doing?"

"I have to go."

"It's two in the morning."

She gave him a wide-eyed look of indifference. "So? I have to go."

"Bree." He touched her arm, the slightest tone of warning in his voice. She yearned to collapse into his arms and stay there all night. If only it were that easy.

"Why do you always do this?" he asked. "You can sleep here, you know."

Why do you always do this?

The words echoed in her mind. He recognized now that she'd never be comfortable enough to stay, and that only increased her urge to leave before she hurt his feelings or did something stupid like start to mourn the fact that they could never have a future.

"I appreciate that, but really...I can't. I had a wonderful time tonight. See you at work."

She blew out the door, leaving him agape behind her.

Every ten minutes, Bree ignored the copy she should have been working on and stared at her open office door. She visualized Evan standing there, his tall and muscular frame filling the doorway, his deceptively commonplace khakis and polo shirt concealing the potent body she knew so intimately.

Over and over again, her mind replayed the scene at his apartment. She could still feel his plush sheets against her skin, see his dark brown eyes looking unabashedly into her soul, smell the cologne that had drifted into her senses when she'd pressed her forehead to his shoulder while he immersed himself inside her. So...deep...inside her.

Oh.

She missed him so much. His sexy grin. That perpetual smirk. The contrast between the brash attitude he displayed in public and the mind-blowing lovemaking he performed behind closed doors.

She had watched, hawk-eyed, all week. It was almost four

o'clock on Thursday afternoon, and every ten minutes she looked.

But he never came.

She couldn't blame him for being mad at her after the way she had left Saturday night. Of course, she'd assumed she would make things right when she saw him Monday. But they weren't working together on anything at the moment—the brochures had been sent to the printer and the website was up to date. Evan had been spending a lot of time in meetings with Paula, and it hadn't occurred to Bree that he would avoid her for so long.

It surprised her how much that hurt.

Her desk phone rang, knocking her out of her reverie and almost her chair. She gathered her composure and picked up the receiver. "Bree Jamison."

"Hi, Bree!"

"Lynn, hey. What's up?"

"You will not believe who I saw today." Her friend gave her a half-second to think of an answer before blurting it out on her own. "I saw *Jeff!*"

Bree clamped her fist around the arm of her chair. She hadn't seen or heard from Jeff since the day she'd booted him out of her apartment.

"Where?" she managed to say, trying not to sound too interested.

"Here at the hospital. With his mega-pregnant girlfriend. She's one of my patients!"

Lynn sounded both aghast at Jeff's affair and excited to be in the middle of the drama. Bree decided not to tell her that Karla was actually the mega-pregnant wife. She didn't want to get into that discussion.

"Wow. I don't know what to say. Did he recognize you?" *Did he mention me,* she wanted to add.

"Yeah, but he just said 'hi' and we pretty much stuck to business. The pregnancy's going smoothly so they weren't in there too long."

In other words, no. Jeff was focused on his new family, not the ex-girlfriend he'd tossed without a second thought. The combination of Lynn's proof that he had moved on and Evan's disturbing absence threatened to bring her lunch back up. She knew her old life was the pits, but when had her new one begun to stink?

"Well, I—" A noise in the hallway caught her attention. "Hold on, Lynn."

She craned her neck and saw Lacy's fiery hair disappear around the corner. A couple of programming guys she didn't know too well bolted past the door in hot pursuit.

"Bree, is everything okay?"

"I'm not sure. Something's going on here. I'll call you later, all right?"

She hung up and crossed the room to peer around the doorjamb. Employees streamed toward the meeting room. Had she missed an announcement? What was going on?

A bad feeling muddied the air. Cautiously, she made her way to the place of interest and poked her head inside. A crowd had gathered around the end of the conference table. She entered the room, feeling Evan's presence immediately and ignoring the moment she saw him out of the corner of her eye. He hung back from the mumbling group and whatever spectacle they hovered over.

She could tell, though, that his arms were crossed and he wasn't pleased. As she stepped closer, a few of her coworkers guiltily looked up from a box full of paper.

She squinted. "Are those the brochures?"

"Yeah." Todd picked up one of the glossy sheets and handed it to her, his voice brimming with annoyance. "See anything you don't like?"

Instantly. She saw it almost as fast as the block of iron plunged into her gut. Right there, on the front of the beautiful brochure she had worked so hard on, the mistake blared at her with its bold red letters: *Paul's Pleasure House.*

Two thousand of the company's most important new promotional materials lay stacked on the table, every one of them spelled wrong.

She swallowed, wanting to cry as well as crumple up the brochures and launch every one of them into the sea of accusing faces. Who in hell was doing this? That thing had been perfect—*perfect*—when she had sent it to the printer. She'd proofread it a hundred times.

"Where's Paula?" she whispered to Todd, trying hard to forget about the dozen other people in the room with them.

Especially the dark-haired figure watching her from the corner.

"In her office. On the phone."

"Has anyone called the printer? I didn't do—"

Todd pulled the order form from his pocket and unfolded it, then held it out in front of her. The printing company claimed to copy text letter for letter, and sure enough, Paula's name was typed incorrectly in the "Text" section of the form.

Bree's fingers trembled into tight fists, her lungs threatening to explode. This wasn't her work. She remembered checking the details right before she'd placed the online order. Someone must have changed the text before the order was processed.

But how? She'd signed in to the vendor's website with a secret password. And would Evan or Todd really turn around and destroy something they'd spent entire days working on?

Whatever was going on, she knew it was personal. No one else's work had been touched. It had been her web page, her brochure. And the theft had taken place on a night *she* had decided to work late.

Who would want to get her fired?

"Evan. Todd. Bree. My office, now." Paula stepped in and out of the conference room in a flash, and she did not sound happy.

Bree had never seen the typically cheerful woman so upset. She finally looked at Evan, who remained stone-faced, and she wished he would offer those reassuring arms that had been so available a few days ago.

Not much chance of that happening. He didn't so much as glance at her as the three of them took seats in front of Paula's desk.

"I'll make this quick." She scrunched her pink locks in her fists before returning her hands to the arms of her chair, her eyes heavy with exhaustion and irritation. "Obviously, something is going on in your department, something that can only be happening from the inside. I'm leaving it up to you three to decide who's responsible."

Bree's heart froze. Overnight, the place she loved and the people she felt so comfortable with had turned dark and cold.

"I don't have time for these games," Paula continued. "I'm sorry, but I want an answer by the end of the day tomorrow or none of you will be guaranteed jobs on Monday."

Evan's face turned a shade of white similar to the one Bree was certain colored her own features. What was he so worried about? Surely he had other clients. She, on the other hand, if she didn't find the elusive culprit, was twenty-four hours away from losing the best thing in her life.

Her job, not her time with Evan. Of course that's what she meant.

After agreeing to meet with Paula again the following evening, the three of them rose from their chairs and filed silently out of her office. When Todd was out of earshot, Bree touched Evan's shoulder. Maybe if they did some amateur sleuthing together, they could figure out what was going on.

"Evan, can we—"

Without looking at her, he raised his hand and kept walking toward his office. "I can't talk right now."

His abrupt words hit her like a slap in the face. Her arm dropped back to her side. She returned to her desk and gathered her things to go home, leaving behind what could very possibly be the worst day of her life.

Until tomorrow.

Chapter Twelve

Evan yanked his starched collar away from his neck and tried to loosen what had begun to feel like a permanently clenched jaw. Eighty degrees and not a cloud in the sky, and he'd smothered his skin in dress pants, a long-sleeved shirt and a too-tight tie.

He scowled into his bathroom mirror. He hated ties. They reminded him of the upper-crust management that had looked down on him since his first job sacking groceries as a fifteen-year-old kid. The stuffy corporate men and women who ignored his lofty GPA and lectured him about the impropriety of his eyebrow ring during post-college job interviews.

He *hated* ties.

Ironically, he wore one today so he would never have to deal with those people again.

Not that his professional appearance would change Paula's mind or guarantee him the top position at PPH. His sister lived for the success of her company, and that success had been threatened. She would do anything to save her business from harm, including suspect—or fire—her own brother.

Or Bree.

The past week had been a nightmare of the loneliest kind. Bree's careless exit last weekend hurt him in ways he didn't understand, ways that irritated the hell out of him. Since when did he throw a pity party if a woman left as soon as they finished having sex? Usually, he preferred it that way. It saved him the trouble of saying awkward goodbyes and offering lame excuses for not seeing a girl again.

But he wanted to see Bree again. And again. The intensity of their lovemaking had made him think she felt something beyond the physical pleasure their bodies provided each other. Maybe she saw past his penniless childhood, his tendency to sarcasm and his unconventional appearance. Unlike any other woman he'd met, maybe she liked his personality and enjoyed his company for something besides sex.

But no. She'd gotten her piece and when he had tried to talk to her about something personal, her reaction had been the same as always.

She had run away. No apology, no explanation, no regrets.

Why couldn't he find his indifferent side when he needed it? Where was the "so what", the "no big deal", the "who cares"? Damn it, he didn't know how he'd let it happen, but he had.

He cared.

He flicked off the bathroom light and grabbed his laptop, determined to get to work as soon as possible. It was fifteen 'til seven, which gave him an hour or two to scour the office for last-minute clues before his sister showed up and started axing jobs.

His phone rang just as he reached the door. He grabbed the receiver off the end table, harboring a small hope that it was Paula calling to say she'd cracked the case. "Hello?"

"Evan."

Though he'd never talked to Bree on the phone, he recognized her voice immediately. When she spoke his name, it stirred up memories of the way she said it while lying naked and breathless in his arms. But this time there was an edge of concern in the sound, and if not for that, he may well have hung up on her.

"What's wrong?"

"Don't panic, but I'm in the emergency room with Paula—"

"What?" He dropped the laptop bag, his fingers a vise around the phone. "What happened? Which hospital?"

She gave him the name, then continued, "She's okay. She fainted, and they want to keep her here a few hours for observation, but I'm sure she'll be home today. I think she was only out for a minute, but she insisted that I bring her—"

"I'm on my way."

Wiping sweat from his brow, he bolted to his car and drove as fast as traffic would allow. Bree could afford the luxury of not panicking, because she didn't know about Paula's condition. What seemed like a simple fainting spell could be anything. The cancer might have spread. Her life could be in danger.

It seemed like a decade passed before he ran into the waiting room of the ER. His gaze darted from patient to patient until he found Bree standing in front of a window, watching dawn break over the half-empty parking lot. He touched her shoulder, and she jumped.

"Oh, Evan. You scared me."

Her green eyes calmed him even in the midst of this crisis. "Where is she?" he asked. "Can I see her?"

"She's in triage, resting. Her doctor's going to check her out and then I think they're going to let her go. I'm so glad I got to the office early today."

At that moment, he noticed the conservative pants and jacket she wore. She continued, "I went in to try to figure out what happened to the brochures before everybody else got there, and I found Paula slumped over her desk. She woke up after a minute and was really disoriented. I don't know what she was doing there so early."

He sighed and sat in one of chairs that lined the wall beneath the window. "Probably the same thing you and I were doing. I was on my way out the door when you called."

"Oh." Her gaze swept over him. "You look really nice."

The compliment caught him off guard. He smoothed his tie and tried to think of an appropriate answer, but it was impossible to keep their relationship casual after everything that had happened between them.

He cleared his throat. "Thanks, you—"

"I'm so sorry I left last weekend." The words tumbled from her lips like she'd held them back far too long. She sat next to him and laid her silky hand on his, and he inhaled the feminine scent of peach lotion. "It's not that I didn't want to be with you, because I did. I do."

She brought his hand to her mouth, leaving a faint lipstick stain on his skin. Tendrils of her hair fell forward and caressed his wrist, and the familiar stirrings of desire sprang into action inside his constrictive clothes. Though he would have liked to hear why she did leave, her apology mattered most. He couldn't bear to face another day without her, especially after she'd acted so quickly to help Paula. If she were the destructive type, would she have done such a thing?

Before he could suppress the urge, he leaned forward and kissed her, tasting the mint flavor of her toothpaste and the desperation of her embrace, a longing that matched his own. She folded her arms tightly around his neck and he ran his hands over her hair, insanely glad their argument had ended.

But before they could make up properly, he needed to check on his sister. He urged Bree to wait for him, and when she promised she wouldn't move from the chair, he asked a nurse to show him to Paula's bed.

The sight alarmed him more than he'd expected, despite the number of awful scenarios that had run through his mind on the way to the hospital. She lay behind a multi-colored curtain, dark circles beneath her half-open eyes. An IV dripped clear fluid into one arm while a blood pressure cuff squeezed the other. He approached her with a heavy heart, fearing terrible news.

Without Paula, he had nothing. She'd been there for him since he was a kid, always finding ways to entertain and distract him from their bleak situation. After Tony died, she had become the only person in the world he trusted. With his parents divorced and living God-knows-where now, she was all the family he had.

What would he do if she were gone?

He claimed a chair next to her bed, shoving that possibility to the furthest corner of his brain. "Is this your way of guilting me into a confession?"

She smiled weakly. "I admit I was trying to bully someone into owning up to this mess, but I know it's not you, Evan. All you've ever wanted is to be your own boss."

"Yeah, well, what I want right now is to know what all this is about." He gestured to the tubes and machines.

She flipped her hand. "It looks worse than it is. I've been working too hard, that's all. Between the cancer and the mysterious vandal, there's too much stress for my body to handle. That's what the doctor on call seems to believe, anyway."

"That's why you fainted? Because of stress?"

"Yeah. I'm not dying yet," she said, humor lacing her voice.

He didn't think it was quite so funny, but he was glad to see her smile. "Not until you're ninety-nine. That was the deal."

"Apparently that's only the deal if I take it easy from now until I finish chemotherapy. You know what that means, don't you?"

"I have to mow your grass and cook all your food?"

"Sure, but first you have to take care of the company. I'm promoting you today. I don't have a choice, and I think you can handle it. Your first task, of course, is to take out the demon in our marketing department."

He couldn't believe his ears. "You're giving me the job now? Your job?"

Paula adjusted her pillow and sat up a bit. Evan almost jumped up to help her, but then he remembered the day she'd given him the news of her diagnosis. She'd made it clear she didn't want to be treated like an invalid, so he kept his butt in the chair while she got comfortable.

"I know it's a big responsibility," she continued. "But you'll have access to everything now—employee records, security logs, you name it. Call the detective and see if he's made any progress. Whatever it takes to end this mess."

He nodded, still trying to comprehend that by the end of the day, he'd be a CEO. How he wished he could take that title to his patronizing teachers and bosses and show them where to shove it. Tony would definitely approve.

Thinking about the tie-wearing community made him reach up and tear apart the careful knot he'd made in his this morning. Paula smiled, and he realized she had to have seen right through his attempt to impress her with his yuppie getup.

"Congratulations," she said. "And if it helps you narrow things down, I'm pretty sure Bree's not involved. I can't imagine why she would have moved so fast to help me this morning if she were."

"I was thinking the same thing."

Just the sound of Bree's name made his heart beat faster. He imagined her waiting for him out by the window. He thought of the way she had saved his sister, and the way she had kissed him a few minutes ago, and his excitement about the job failed.

It didn't make sense. He should have been thrilled—his lifelong dream was coming true.

But living that dream would bring his relationship with Bree to an end, and somehow, that only made him feel empty.

"Okay, folks!" Clapping her hands, Paula entered the room in a rush of pink hair, purple leather and strong perfume, her rambunctious spirit alive and well. "Settle down and pay attention, because we've got a lot of things to cover."

Bree snuck a peek at Evan, who sat at the other end of the conference table near his sister. He flashed her a wink and a smile that melted her panties and her heart. She thanked heaven that Paula's fainting episode hadn't been critical. Her regular doctor had checked her out and released her after just two hours. Now it was a matter of finding out if they would all still have jobs at the end of the day.

"There's something we need to discuss, something a bit serious." Paula took a breath and released it slowly. "Several weeks ago, I was diagnosed with stage one lymphoma. I'll be out for an extended period of time for treatment and—"

Audible gasps interrupted her announcement. Several members of the staff, most of whom had been friends with Paula for years, rose from their chairs and made moves to approach her, not even waiting to hear what else she had to say. Bree raised her fingers to her lips, unable to imagine such a bright, dynamic woman being slowed down by the effects of cancer.

She glanced at Evan, wanting to go to him and help him through this hard time. His expression was staunch, glum—but not surprised. Of course not. Paula would have told her brother long before she gave the news to her employees.

"Please, everybody." Paula held up her hands and motioned for the group to remain seated. "I appreciate your concern, I really do. And I'll be happy to talk with you about my condition later, but there's going to be a big change here, and I need your full cooperation."

Paula exchanged a look with Evan, who stood up and joined her in front of the expectant crowd. With a nervous smile, she took his arm. "I'm glad this one decided to dress up today, because his look fits the part. I want to introduce you to the man who will be your new CEO effective Monday morning."

The world came to a screeching halt.

Her new *what*?

"I apologize for misleading you," her boss—for the time being—went on. "Evan is a successful marketing consultant and has been for six years, but there was a more important reason I brought him on here. I wanted to gauge how well you would all work together while I'm away, and I'm so thankful for how easily you've come to accept him."

Dampness shone in Paula's brown eyes. "I promise, he will change nothing about the way things are run here. He's well-versed on my policies."

She grinned at him, a sassy yet grateful smirk, and members of the group offered congratulations. Evan smiled and thanked them, but when Bree dared to look at him, she caught him watching her. She shifted her focus to the yellow flower adorning Paula's lapel. The last thing she wanted to see now were those deep cocoa eyes she'd come to know, to desire...to trust.

It pained her to question that trust, but Evan's meager reaction to the news of his promotion proved it wasn't news to him at all. He knew he hadn't been hired as a marketing consultant and that Paula had planned to turn the company over to him. Most likely, he also knew that to earn the CEO position, he would have to fit in with the employees.

All of the employees. Including her.

Who had hated him more than she did when he'd first arrived at PPH? She would have given her right arm to get rid of him, and he couldn't have been blind to that fact.

She watched with growing trepidation as the meeting ended and her coworkers milled around consoling Paula and questioning Evan. He had seduced her. He'd seduced her because he sensed her attraction to him and that had paved his route to her acceptance. And how could she blame him? She had enjoyed every breathtaking minute of it.

She closed her eyes. It was five o'clock. The next time she stepped foot in that office, Evan would be her boss.

Her adventure was over.

Michelle hovered in a vacant corner of the lobby, her hand clamped around her cell phone when she should have been in the conference room with everyone else.

"You know Paula ended up in the hospital this morning?" she snapped at Harry. "This has gotten out of hand. We're stopping this thing now."

"I'm sorry, but you haven't delivered your end of the deal yet."

"And I won't. You've completely lost sight of the point. Just because you can lock yourself in the darkness of your room and screw with other people's lives through the computer doesn't mean you should."

"Well, well. If the deal is off, then I guess I'm not doing this for you anymore. I'm just having fun, and therefore I have no obligation to stop."

Her heart pounded, his statement confirming her fear that his disturbing personality had moved into the realm of madness. "I swear, if you do one more—"

He laughed. "What? What are you gonna do?"

Sadly, she couldn't think of an answer.

"That's what I thought," he spat. "You can't do shit, so go screw a married guy or something. And don't expect me to bail you out anymore. Your company is my video game, and I'm holding the controls now."

"Harry!" she pleaded, but he hung up on her.

Chapter Thirteen

Evan wondered what in hell was wrong with him.

His goal of running his own business, the one thing he'd wanted his entire life, had been realized that afternoon. He should have been partying, whooping it up at Barry's or some place equally filled with alcohol and gorgeous, lustful ladies who could help him celebrate his good fortune.

Instead, he was standing on Bree's doorstep. At nine o'clock at night. With a bunch of daisies in his hand.

At some point, he'd transformed into either a sissy or an upstanding gentleman who did things like buy flowers for a woman he had spent more than a day with. A woman he couldn't stop thinking about even when he knew good and well that his time with her would be over at eight-thirty on Monday morning.

Maybe that's why he badly needed one more night with her.

"Did you follow me home?"

He blinked, seeing that Bree had opened the door while he'd been poised there dreaming about her. One of her hands clutched the collar of a panting, flaxen dog. The other scraped through her hair.

"No, I saw the address on that baby gift the other day." He also had access to each employee's personal information now, but he didn't want to remind her of his new title.

Uncomfortable silence ensued, so he offered her the bouquet. "Word on the street says buying a woman flowers can earn forgiveness for acting like an ass."

A surprised half-smile lit her face, though her eyes remained wary and her long look at his expression judged his level of sincerity. "You didn't have to do that."

"Can I come in?"

"Um...sure, okay." Pinching her lips together, she opened the door wider and let him inside, then closed it and set the dog free.

"He's friendly," Evan commented, petting the top of the dog's head.

"She. Her name's Ginger."

"Ah. Sorry, girl."

Ginger licked his hand in forgiveness while Bree arranged the flowers in a vase of water and then paced around with her back to him. He didn't see any bras, tampons or dirty underwear occupying the floor of her immaculate apartment, so why did she look so nervous?

He hadn't gotten a chance to talk to her after the meeting. His coworkers had blitzed him with questions and comments about the upcoming transition, most of them positive, to his relief, and Bree had disappeared at some point during the chaos. Not exactly shocking, since he knew all too well how often she ran away from her problems. Especially when they involved him.

She stuck her hands in her hair again, vanishing into the kitchen. "Can I get you a drink? Anything? I'm sorry I'm such a mess. I wasn't expecting anyone."

Only then did he figure out why she kept a careful distance between them. He crossed through her living room and leaned against the kitchen counter, taking a good, long look at her that made her cringe. She wore navy sweatpants and a plain white

152

T-shirt that hugged her full breasts and narrow waist. Her hair smelled freshly washed and fell loosely around her jaw line, and her face was beautifully clean. He'd never seen her without makeup before, and the sight of her so...*naked*, in a sense, without her sexy façade to hide behind, made him want her more than ever.

"What are you talking about? You look great."

She waved her hand and rolled her eyes. "Please. Flattery isn't necessary, I already let you in."

Their eyes locked. She wet her lips, and he grew intensely aware of the closeness of their bodies, separated by nothing but a few inches of granite.

"Well," she continued in a soft but formal tone. "Thank you very much for the flowers. What can I do for you, Evan? Can I still call you Evan? Or is it 'sir' now?"

Yeah...she was pissed.

He took a deep breath for the purpose of relieving stress, but instead he inhaled a sweet floral scent that emanated from Bree's skin. "You smell good."

"I hope so. I just got out of the shower."

Oh, man. How easily his mind created an image of Bree in the shower with him, hot water dripping down their entwined bodies as he kissed her wet lips, held her up against the tiled wall and pushed deep inside her.

Right. At that moment she would slap him silly before she'd let him touch her like that.

"Bree, I'm sorry. I couldn't tell you because Paula wasn't ready to tell anyone about her health yet—"

"You don't have to explain anything to me. I mean, we were just screwing, right? That's what we do. No big deal."

Now she sounded like him. Him before he met *her*.

"Don't do that. Please don't disregard everything we've

shared."

"Were we sharing something? Or was that your unique way of convincing me to like you so I wouldn't get in the way of your new job?"

He rounded the counter and stared her down. "Stop. I made love to you because I wanted to. Period. I was under the impression that you wanted it, too."

Her gaze dropped. "I did."

"So we shared something. Something special."

"It doesn't matter what we shared, Evan. What matters is that next week you're going to be my boss. The freaking president of the company, for God's sake. I'm sure I'd be stepping on some toes if I were sleeping with you."

"I know we have to stop." He waited a beat before plunging ahead with his proposition. "On Monday."

The hunger reflected in her emerald eyes inspired passionate thoughts of giving her a goodbye she'd never forget. "What are you suggesting?" she demanded.

He stepped closer. "Be with me. Tonight. Make love with me so long and so hard that neither of us will be able to move tomorrow."

That last comment appeared to throw her off balance. Her startled expression reminded him that she still had so much to experience, and he desperately wanted to play the role of her sensual tour guide.

He looked down at her, amused that the top of her head barely reached his jaw when she wasn't wearing shoes that resembled sharp weaponry. "Tell me you didn't mean what you said. Tell me we weren't just screwing."

She took his hand and ran feather-light touches over his fingers, exploring his rough digits with her own soft and slender ones. "We weren't."

Her entranced movements set his flesh on fire. "How do I make you feel?"

"You make me feel..." She closed her eyes. "Do you really think I look okay?"

He gaped. Did she think she needed all that short, tight garb to look good? No doubt, she was sexy as hell dressed up, but this pure, *real* glimpse of her had his cock rigid and his veins sizzling, not to mention the inexplicable desire he felt to curl up with her and hold her close to him all night long.

"You look beautiful," he answered honestly.

She held him in front of her, moving her palms over his shirt sleeves and shoulders. He shivered when she cradled the back of his neck and gently dragged her nails through his hair.

"Do you mind if I just look at you?"

His heart rate picked up speed. He'd been with a lot of women, and not one of them had asked for such a thing. They had kept busy taking what they'd come for—nameless, faceless sex. Bree's simple request suggested something personal and highly intimate. The kind of thing that tended to give him the urge to flee.

But his feet were firmly planted on the tile of her kitchen floor.

"What's on your mind?" he managed to say. Her touch posed a serious threat to his self-control.

She shook her head. "I just can't believe you're the same guy I couldn't stand."

Evan thought back to that very first night when their paths had crossed with such disastrous results. Odd, but he could hardly remember what life felt like when he didn't have Bree to think about every day. "First impressions aren't very accurate, you know. You've changed a dozen times since the day we met."

"I have?"

"Let's see. First I thought you were looking for cheap sex like every other woman who's hit on me in a bar. Then I thought you were a timid virginal thing, and then a conceited snob. Now I see a beautiful, kind, sexy woman I'm very lucky to know."

She blinked, playing with her hair again. "Wow. Well, I guess this is the real me. The whore-in-the-bar look was a creation of Jessica. She also told me to leave your apartment after the one-night stand without saying goodbye."

"She did what?"

"Well, I called her when you were in the shower. She told me you wouldn't mind because you probably did that kind of stuff all the time."

He held back a laugh, though the words came too close to the truth. He used to settle for one-night stands because he had no idea how amazing long hours of meaningful sex could be. After the passion he'd experienced with Bree, the thought of going back to his bar-hopping days twisted his insides into a regretful knot.

Amusement tugged at the corner of her mouth. "I think I just blew my cover. If I were used to picking up strange men and demanding that they satisfy me, I probably wouldn't have needed so much help that night."

Evan chuckled and led her to the sofa, where Ginger approached and lay down at their feet. Despite Bree's early attempt to blame their botched night together on him, it was clear her weird parents and dimwitted ex had caused her far more pain. "I'm pretty sure I had you figured out already. But for the record, are you saying I'm not a loser in bed after all?"

She blushed. "I'm afraid I was the loser. I shouldn't have listened to Jess. One-night stands are her thing, not mine."

"Why are you so dependent on those girlfriends of yours?"

"They're my best friends. I trust them."

"But you turn to them for all your dating advice. Don't you

trust yourself?"

"Should I? My last boyfriend wouldn't even consider getting engaged after spending three years with me, but two seconds later he's married to someone else. That doesn't say much about my dating skills."

"All it says is that he's a dickhead. And you deserve better." He leaned in close and kissed her. "You're jaded, Bree. Forget getting back at Jeff. Forget being like your friends. You're sexy just the way you are."

Chapter Fourteen

Bree's neck hurt and her mouth tasted like she'd filled it with cotton balls. Her eyes half open, she rolled over and threw her arm across a pillow that took a deep breath and mumbled something in its sleep.

Wait a minute...

Forcing her lids completely up, she lifted her head and inspected the last scene she ever thought she'd see. Evan lay face-up on her sofa, his arm around her shoulder, her body draped over his leg and one side of his torso. The kitchen light gleamed from around the corner and they still wore their clothes and shoes, having apparently fallen asleep in the middle of last night's conversation.

The window blinds remained shrouded in darkness, and she craned her neck to see the digital clock on her microwave. Five a.m. A stinging sensation warned her that she needed to get up and squirt some eye drops on the contacts she'd left in all night, but she couldn't turn away from Evan's peaceful slumber.

She propped up on her elbow and absorbed the sight of him. He wore blue jeans and a light gray T-shirt in place of the usual black. Tufts of his dark hair pressed against the cushion of her cream-colored sofa where his head rested. She listened to the soft sound of his breathing and watched his eyelids flutter as he dreamed.

She reached out and slowly, barely touched her finger to the silver ring over his eye, the part of him that had caught her attention in the first place. She had despised him for the vulgarity it symbolized, then wanted him for the adventure it promised. Now she knew his character reached far deeper than either of those oversimplified roles, but that didn't stop her from wanting to continue their illicit affair.

His promotion to CEO and the end of their liaison would be the best thing that could happen to her. Thanks to her accomplishment of the kinky items on Jessica's list, she no longer felt useless between the sheets. Now she needed to stop playing around and start looking for someone to fill the position Jeff had left vacant. Tempting though Evan's delicious body and intriguing personality were, his casual approach to relationships made him fling material. He was fun. Sex. Nothing more.

So why hadn't she remembered to kick him out before they'd fallen asleep in each other's arms?

With a resigned sigh, she removed herself from Evan and the sofa and stumbled into the bathroom to wet her painfully dry contacts. She squeezed a stream of drops into her eyes and closed them, feeling the cool relief spread behind her lids. She blinked a few times, and when she opened her eyes again, she looked into the mirror and straight into Evan's gaze.

"Hey." His voice cracked and the corner of his mouth turned up.

She gave him a shaky smile, unsure how he would react to the knowledge that he'd spent the night at her place. "I guess we fell asleep."

He stretched his arms over his head and rolled his shoulders and back. "Yeah, sleeping in jeans isn't the most comfortable thing in the world. That's why I took them off."

She turned and sure enough, he stood there clad in only a

pair of navy blue boxers. The butterflies in her stomach multiplied.

"I was wondering if I could use your shower." He strolled to the glass door, pulled it open and turned on the faucet.

She couldn't find enough words to form a sentence. His bare chest and morning hair had destroyed her ability to speak.

He glanced at his watch before slipping it off and setting it beside the sink. "You probably need to get in yourself, don't you? We have a busy day ahead of us."

They didn't have a thing planned for the day, and she knew what kind of activities he intended. A sudden rush of wetness poured into a place far away from her freshly moistened eyes.

She just nodded.

"Well, then." He flashed her a provocative smile. "Come on in."

Her jaw fell and she couldn't tear her gaze away as he dropped his boxers to the floor and stepped into the hot spray. He winked at her before closing the door, which blurred the enticing view of his bare backside she'd been enjoying. Good Girl Bree tried to convince her to leave him be and go back to the living room, but New Bree understood that if she didn't have him now, she'd never have him again. And she wasn't ready to give up her adventure just yet.

Monday morning crept ever closer.

She stripped and approached the shower. She'd always heard that guys jacked off in there, but Evan must have seen no need for that, knowing she would join him. He leaned against the small white tiles, his cross-armed stance and irresistible grin a portrait of machismo.

"I've been expecting you."

Her uncertainty gone, she bit back a smile and lifted one foot, then the other, over the threshold and into the warm mist.

She didn't hesitate before stepping close to him and running her hands over his strong, wet chest.

"You make me feel sexy. You make me feel things I didn't know were possible," she said in answer to last night's question.

His lips grazed her neck while he backed her into the water and raked his fingers through her hair so she emerged wet from head to toe. The smooth friction of their skin astounded her. The upright position of her body sent her blood racing downward and pooling between her legs quicker than usual, rendering her wobbly on her feet. Evan held her steady, one hand against her back, the other cradling her butt while they kissed themselves breathless, and his erection pressed mercilessly against her abdomen.

He picked up the slick bar of soap and glided it along her arms and back, his movements slow and deliberate as though he caressed her with his own fingertips. "You've never felt passion before."

He stated it as a fact, and she couldn't disagree. "No."

"Do you feel it now?"

"I feel it every time I'm with you."

She took the bar and skimmed it across his torso while he rubbed the lather over her slippery skin. They rinsed off the soap and he held her against the wall, trailing his hand down her side. She kissed him and scraped her fingers through the damp hair on his chest. His thumb brushed her clit and she whimpered, dropping her head and running her tongue over his neck and shoulder. She nearly bit him when he placed two fingers against her swollen, primed opening and pressed them into her body.

"There are so many ways, Bree. So many..."

She moaned and closed her eyes. The swish of running water, the rousing sound of Evan's sweet nothings, and the rhythm of his touch all at once probing inside her and stroking her insanely sensitive sex made her feel as though she'd entered another world. Oh, God, she was going to do it. She was going to come, too fast, too soon...

She shattered. Colors and patterns flashed behind her closed lids and her legs gave way, her shouts bouncing off the bathroom walls. He supported her weight between his body and the wall, not slowing his caress until he'd squeezed another round of pleasure out of her.

Catching her breath, she sank to her knees and curled her lips over his cock, teasing him with the swirling motion of her tongue. He exhaled noisily, and she relished the knowledge that she was capable of pleasing him so well. Evan, who had slept with so many experienced women, was turned on by *her*—a conservative goody-two-shoes.

He made her feel so happy, so complete. And she wanted to give back to him all the enjoyment he provided her.

"Bree," he groaned, cupping the back of her head with his hand. "*Stop.* I can't wait—"

"You don't have to." Her actions grew more intense.

"Are you sure?"

She took him out of her mouth, and deft strokes of her hand brought him over the edge. He slapped his palm against the side of the shower. The warmth of his release coated her breasts, and she rested her head against his stomach for a long, blissful moment before standing and rinsing off in the water.

When she was finished, Evan reached around her and shut off the faucet. He reached outside the door and grabbed a large towel from a chrome rack, wrapping it securely around her shoulders.

She looked at him with awed eyes and a sated smile, like they'd just made love for the first time. He returned her smile and kissed her forehead, still reeling from what she had done to him.

"Come to bed with me," he said.

He followed her to her bedroom, where she surprised him again by pulling a condom from her bedside drawer, climbing atop his hips and easing him into her body.

He buried his face beneath her chin, breathing in her scent and stroking the soft skin of her neck in awe at their union. He never knew need could be so powerful or reach the level of intensity it did when he made love with Bree. She induced feelings in him that he couldn't define, could hardly even bear. Every time he looked at her—every time he thought of her—his heart felt like it would burst right through his skin, and that nervous sensation subsided only when he was deep inside her.

"I want to stay this way forever," she whispered, rocking slowly against him. "It's like I'm addicted to you."

Evan caught his breath. He doubted she knew the truth of her words. Unfortunately, she was addicted to sex with him— not *him*. He'd seen it a million times. Whenever he went to a club, ladies approached him looking for a night away from their boring careers and sensible lives. Getting busy with a bad boy played a part in every woman's fantasy, or so he'd read in a girlie magazine Paula had shown him a few years back just to prove it wasn't his charm getting him so many dates.

He wished Bree were a different story. He wished she wanted to be a part of his life outside the bedroom. But he'd heard from her own mouth the story of her grandiose parents and the puritanical life she'd been forced to live. She worked at PPH to escape that life, and she slept with him to escape it.

Not that any of that mattered, because he was forty-eight hours away from being her boss and he couldn't have her, anyway.

"That could be dangerous," he teased, turning his attention back to the erotic vision in his arms.

"You're not dangerous."

She held him tighter and he buried his floored expression in her sweet-smelling hair as they found a rhythm and carried each other to ecstasy. He wasn't? What was she doing to his tough-guy image?

And why didn't he mind?

Between alternating bouts of sleep and sex, it was almost noon by the time Bree downed a glass of orange juice and watched Evan clean up the breakfast he'd insisted on making for them. While he'd cooked, she had brushed her teeth, put on light makeup, and dressed in jeans and a red baby tee. Her hair was dry and nicely tousled, and she felt gorgeous.

Evan's lovemaking had that effect on her.

She didn't know why she allowed them to sit around and play house when she should have shown him the door a long time ago. With every passing minute he became further ingrained in her life and her emotions, a fact that would only make it that much harder for her to distance herself from him come Monday.

"So, how did everybody take the news of your promotion?" she asked brightly, trying to get in the habit of discussing business with him.

He wiped his hands on a towel and sat next to her at the table, his shirtless torso tucked into stonewashed denim. "No big deal. Most of them were her friends before they were her employees, anyway. They understand that she does what's best for the company."

"I can't believe her diagnosis. I'm so sorry, Evan. I really hope her treatment is successful."

"She'll be okay. She's tough."

The doorbell rang and Bree jumped from her chair to

escape a conversation way too stilted to take place with a man who had spent half the night inside her. She opened the door just in time to notice a man in a brown uniform retreating down the stairs. She stiffened when she saw the large box on top of her welcome mat.

"Not again." She dragged it inside and shut the door, not even bothering to open the package. Jeff's name on the label told her everything she needed to know.

She stalked back into the kitchen, yanked the white pages out of a cabinet and flipped through them, then tossed the book aside and plucked the cordless phone from its cradle. She punched a few numbers. No answer.

"Damn it!" She bashed the phone on the counter.

"Can I help?"

Evan didn't touch her, just stood nearby and let her know he was there. She cursed again, this time silently. She could handle the inevitable end of their affair if he provided her with nothing but hot sex. Why did he have to be so sensitive? So compassionate, so caring?

She shook her head. "I can't avoid this any longer. I have to see him."

"Who? That numb nuts, Jeff?

"Yeah."

"Why on earth would you want to see him?"

Was that jealousy flaring in his eyes?

"I didn't say I want to." She pressed her fingertips into the countertop as if that would relieve her headache. "I *have* to."

Evan rolled his eyes, but his voice was soft. "Excuse me for misunderstanding. Why do you *have* to see him?"

"Look at the size of that gift. I can't just throw this stuff out. Somebody spent a lot of money on this."

"That's not your problem."

"No, but—"

The phone rang, and she snatched it up. "Lynn, thank God. Why didn't you answer your cell phone?"

"I'm working the after-hours clinic. What's the emergency?"

"You're at work? Awesome. I need Jeff's address. You know, his pregnant wife is your patient? You have access to that information, right?"

"So you know she's his wife. I didn't want to say anything."

"It doesn't matter. I just need the address. Now."

Bree never knew silence could be so irritating.

"That's confidential stuff," her friend finally answered. "I don't think I'm supposed to—"

"*Please*, Lynn. I'm not asking for their social security numbers and access to their checking account. Just an address. Please. I keep getting their baby gifts and I need to send them back."

Lynn spoke quietly, as though talking to a child or a recently incarcerated mental patient. "Bree, have you tried the phone book?"

She stared at the ceiling. "Yes! They're not listed."

A heavy sigh sounded over the line. "Fine. Just this once. Don't you dare tell anyone I gave you this information."

"I promise I won't."

Lynn gave her the address and Bree scribbled it on a notepad, then thanked her and hung up. Evan stood behind her, his shirt on and his arms crossed. "There you go. You can mail the packages back and be done with it."

"I'm not mailing them. I'm going over there. Today."

Chapter Fifteen

Evan questioned his decision the moment they pulled away from Bree's apartment building. He'd insisted on going with her, supposedly because he didn't want her to drive riled up and he wanted to provide support if seeing Jeff in the flesh ended up being too hard on her.

Of course, that was bullshit. At the least, it wasn't the whole truth. He really wanted to go because he couldn't stand the thought of her being alone with her ex-boyfriend—or any other man, for that matter.

Now that they were on the road and he could think straight again, it occurred to him that she wouldn't be alone with Jeff. His nine-months-pregnant wife would be at the house and maybe even in labor. What business did Evan have showing up at the home of these people he didn't even know, and at such an important time in their lives?

He felt he had come to know them, through their association with Bree. He was in deep. Way too deep.

How would he survive seeing her at work every day? Especially the way she dressed there. She would flaunt every luscious curve right in front of his face day in and day out. He'd spend hours walking the same floor where they made love for the first time—the real first time. The vast collection of sex toys scattered around the office would only serve to remind him of the ways they had pleased each other with those gadgets.

And he would be absolutely, positively, no exceptions forbidden to date her.

After a few weeks of seeing her nearly every day, he'd finally admitted to himself that he wanted to date her. Granted, he wanted to continue sleeping with her, but he also wanted time to enjoy her sense of humor and sharp wit, take her to dinner, hold her hand in a movie theater like they were sixteen. Time to talk with her and watch the movements of her beautiful eyes and mouth as she spoke. To learn more about her, and show her more about him.

He racked his brain for a way to make it work, but no solution seemed feasible. They would have to work in separate offices, and both of them needed their positions at PPH too much to give that up. And then there was the fact that he couldn't be sure Bree wanted him for anything other than a distraction from her strait-laced past, not to mention her plans to someday have a wedding. Just the word scared the shit out of him.

No wonder he avoided relationships. They were too damned complicated. His inner playboy needed to come back to life, and fast.

"That's the street, right there." Bree's fraught voice cut into his thoughts, bringing his attention back to their unpleasant situation.

She pointed to his left, and reluctantly he made the turn. "Are you sure you want to do this?"

"I don't have a choice. It's about more than the boxes."

So...what? This journey of self-discovery would get her over Jeff for good? Profound, but not likely. Evan didn't welcome the scenario that would unfold even if she did let go of her anger. Most likely, when she resolved her issues with her ex, she wouldn't need a rough-around-the-edges guy like him to sex her up on a regular basis. She would realize that she'd been fine living her conventional life before her heart had been broken, and she'd go back to looking for Mr. 'Til Death Do Us Part.

Evan Willett was not that man.

He parked next to the curb and gazed at the single-story brick house, admiring its nicely landscaped yard. The place was big and well-kept, and on the outside it looked like Jeffrey and Karla Warner enjoyed a happy and comfortable life. Recalling Bree's mental breakdown in her office after Baby Package Number One, Evan hoped she'd be able to cope.

"Thanks. I'll be right back." She got out of the car and rifled around in the backseat, stacking the smaller box on top of the large one before hauling them both to the front door.

He folded his hands and rested them on the steering wheel. He could only imagine what the next few minutes would bring.

The lump in Bree's throat tripled in size when she heard footsteps approaching the oak door. In reality it had only been about half a minute since she'd knocked, but the tornadic spinning of her stomach prolonged every second. The urge to punch Jeff in his dishonest mouth had subsided, but she wasn't exactly raring to see him again—or meet the woman he'd slept with behind her back.

Knowing Evan waited a few feet away seemed to help. Though she had protested when he'd insisted on coming with her, the closer they'd gotten to Jeff's house, the more grateful she felt that she didn't have to do this alone.

She had no idea what had inspired her goodwill. She should have tossed the gifts or sent them back to the post office. But her playtime with Evan was nearly over, and she needed to be ready to start fresh. She needed to look for someone to build a relationship and a future with.

That meant letting go of her past, and facing Jeff was the only way to do that.

But when the door opened, it wasn't Jeff who stared back at her. A short young woman with a curly ponytail smiled expectantly. "Can I help you?"

Bree waited for the surge of anger and pain she expected, but it didn't come. Maybe it was Karla's friendly tone, or the huge, round belly weighing down her petite frame, but Bree couldn't seem to reconcile her with the boyfriend-stealing witch she'd imagined for all these months. She looked, and looked again, but she saw only a nice, pretty girl excitedly awaiting the arrival of her first child.

"I—you must be Karla." Bree stumbled over her words, trying to grasp her shock at her benevolent feelings.

"Yes. Have we met?"

Gesturing to the cardboard boxes on the porch, Bree decided to go with the direct approach since she hadn't at all planned what she would say once she arrived. "No. Not yet. Actually, I'm Jeff's ex-girlfriend. Some of his relatives don't have your new address, and they've sent a few baby things to my place."

Karla's mouth formed an O and her eyes widened as though she knew Bree and Jeff's relationship hadn't ended on the best of terms. "Oh, my God. I'm so sorry. Bree, right?"

Surprised, she nodded.

"Oh, no, I can't believe this. I really am sorry. You didn't have to—thank you for bringing them over. That's incredibly sweet of you."

"Well, I figured you might need this stuff. Congratulations, by the way."

Unbelievable. She almost felt happy for this woman. For Jeff's *wife*.

Karla smiled and waved her inside. "Would you mind helping me out with the tall one? I think it's too big for me to..." Her voice trailed off and she looked down at her tummy, putting

170

one hand over her protruding navel.

"Of course." Bree exchanged a look with Evan, who watched the drama unfold from behind the car window. He rolled his eyes, undoubtedly amused that two women who should have been mortal enemies were chattering like best friends. *Whatever,* he mouthed. Bree stepped into Karla's foyer, choosing to ignore that the house also belonged to Jeff.

"Jeff's not here," the younger woman said, reading her mind. "He ran out to put gas in the car because this one's coming out any day now."

She paused, then looked up at Bree with sadness in her eyes. "I just want to apologize for everything you've been through. I didn't mean to cause you any pain. Jeff swore he was going to tell you and we weren't expecting..." She glanced at her expanding abdomen again.

"Don't apologize." Bree placed a hand on the tall box to support her legs, which threatened to collapse. Jeff had actually mentioned her? Told Karla her name as though she were a human being, maybe even one with feelings?

"It wasn't your fault. And I'm doing fine. I've met someone I'm very happy with, and I'm glad you and Jeff are happy, too."

She meant every word. She couldn't believe it. When she'd said the whole bit about having met someone, she had intended it as a fib so Karla wouldn't feel guilty. But as soon as the words left her mouth, she knew they were true. Evan made her happy. Happier than she had ever been, even back when she and Jeff had first gotten together.

She didn't want to lose him, and the thought of being nothing more than his employee shot a wave of nausea down her throat.

The sound of shouting from outside sent the two women scurrying back out the front door. The open garage revealed a black SUV that Jeff had just parked and next to it, the old white sports car he'd owned since before Bree met him. She took in his familiar blond hair and lean frame and felt little emotion—quite the opposite of what happened when she turned her head and saw Evan storming up the driveway, fists clenched.

"Evan, stop!"

"Bree?" Jeff looked startled but didn't have time to dwell on the feeling, because Evan paid no heed to her request and continued his path of fury toward the younger—and smaller—man.

A small gasp escaped Karla's throat, and Bree sensed a huge disaster in the works. Surely Evan didn't plan to beat Jeff senseless because of her, did he?

"Evan!" she called again, this time running to his side and yanking his arm. "What are you doing?"

Jeff took the opportunity to step out of Evan's path and put a reassuring arm around Karla's shoulder. "If that's your psychotic boyfriend, take him home. He jumped out of his car as soon as I got here and—"

"You want to talk psychotic?" Evan's eyes neared bulging, along with a vein on his forehead. "How about running someone over and driving away? You killed my best friend, you bastard."

Evan wanted to throw up when he laid eyes on the same white Porsche he'd watched speed into the distance after it had tossed Tony down the street like a rag doll. He could still hear the muted sound of the engine roaring as he'd knelt next to his friend's body and begged him not to die.

God, he didn't want it to be true. He would rather spend the rest of his life ignorant to the identity of his friend's killer than know that Bree's former lover had been the one behind the wheel. He wanted to find out that he was mistaken, that he'd overreacted when the garage door opened, but he knew that car. He'd never forget that car. Its image had been permanently burned into his mind the moment it took Tony out of his life forever. It obviously belonged to one of the two occupants of the house, and from the looks of her, Karla wouldn't have been old enough to drive ten years ago.

The only other option, then, was the man he intended to pound into the concrete.

Jeff's face grew pale. "What are you talking about?"

"I suppose you don't remember," Evan snarled. "How old were you—seventeen, eighteen?"

"Enough." Bree stepped between the two of them, her tone sharp. "We need to go."

"Why? Don't you want to know what a blessing it is that he left you? Your precious loverboy is a cold-blooded—"

"Can we talk about this somewhere else?" she interrupted loudly. Her gaze burned into his, her voice a near-plea.

He realized then that it probably wasn't the best idea to burst out with something so serious in front of Karla, who looked about ten seconds away from giving birth. "Fine. Let's go."

He pointed at Jeff. "You can expect a call from the pol—"

Bree grabbed his arm for the second time. "Not here," she growled, escorting him to the passenger seat of his car and leaving Jeff and Karla dumbfounded in their front yard.

Evan sulked in the seat, staring at the dashboard and not giving a damn that Bree had taken his keys. She started the engine and inched through the residential streets. He couldn't think of a thing to say to her. He felt like he didn't even know her anymore, and maybe he never had.

"I haven't seen him drive that car, not once." She broke the silence after they turned out of Jeff's neighborhood. "He just keeps it so he can show it off."

She sounded optimistic about the guy's innocence.

Irritated, Evan found his voice. "How long has he had it?"

"His dad bought it for him when he turned sixteen."

"And when was that?"

She appeared to be calculating in her head. "Nineteen ninety-eight."

"Tony died in ninety-nine. I imagine Jeff was still playing with his new toy at that point."

Bree didn't answer, which told him she couldn't deny the possibility.

He rested his elbow against the window and cradled his forehead, squeezing his eyes closed. *She slept with him.* The sickening thought filled the interior of the car like a thick fog. It seeped into his nostrils, poured down his throat, and wrapped around his neck. Squeezing him. Choking him.

"Stop the car."

She flicked her gaze in his direction before turning back to the road. "What? Where?"

"Anywhere. Just stop." Never mind the fact that they were in the middle of a busy street. He needed breathing room, and time to think. Time to forget about the feelings he'd been harboring for Bree and the hours they'd spent in her bed that very morning.

She pulled into a small rest area. The instant she killed the engine, Evan jumped outside and paced a narrow gravel path. The sound of a slamming door jolted his attention away from the dusty white rocks and back to the woman he wasn't sure whether to love or hate.

She leaned against the hood, keys in hand. "What are you planning to do?"

His chest tightened as he studied the denim-clad curves adorning the front of his vehicle. Her quiet question went right to the point, sparing him the interrogation about what had happened that awful night and how he could be sure Jeff was the guilty party. She believed him, trusted his judgment—and that made him appreciate her even more.

But it didn't matter now. They had already been headed toward the end of their affair, and this new development only cemented its demise.

"Call the police," he answered. "In fact, I should do that right now." He unclipped his cell phone from his belt, but Bree moved toward him and placed her hand over his.

"Do you have to?"

He stared, aghast. "What do you mean, do I have to? Of course I have to! He killed somebody. That's no minor offense."

"No, but..."

Damn it, anyway. Maybe she wasn't on his side, after all.

"Tell me you're not defending him just because of your relationship with him."

"I don't have a relationship with him," she countered. "I'm not defending him. But if he's guilty, he'll go to jail for God knows how long. That baby will grow up without a father."

"And I'm supposed to care about that?"

He realized too late how harsh those words sounded. Bree wore a devastated expression, undoubtedly brought on by the fact that he had just made himself out to be a heartless jerk.

She whispered an answer. "I thought you might."

He hated that look in her eyes, one that made him feel like he'd stolen a little kid's security blanket. He didn't want to hurt her, but she didn't understand.

She would never understand.

She and Jeff belonged to the same world. A world where everything could be solved with money or connections, where image and reputation mattered more than family and friends. Where a person with enough social clout could get away with murder.

Bree had *loved* Jeff—a man capable of killing someone and casually going on with his life, never looking back. She'd loved him, lived with him, made love to him...day after day, year after year. Because before he cheated on her, he was Mr. Rich, Mr. Med Student, Mr. Upper Crust.

Mr. Right.

It wasn't enough for her that Evan wanted her even on her worst day. It wasn't enough that he'd shown her passion, life and adventure. She still used him for sex and then insisted they go their separate ways. He'd only been at her place that morning because they had accidentally fallen asleep. Before that package had shown up at her door, he could tell she'd been minutes away from asking him to leave.

Again, his mind flooded with memories of their recent lovemaking. But then he saw Jeff kissing her, Jeff's hands on her...

Jeff's hands, stained with Tony's blood and with Bree's love. That bastard had taken everything from him.

"I'm not defending Jeff," she repeated, placing her hand on his arm. "I don't care about him. I care about you."

He shrugged her off, his mind still spinning. The day had turned into a colossal mess and he had no idea how to handle any of it.

"But Karla and the baby. As much as I hate to say this, they need him. The baby—"

"I understand that there's a baby, Bree. But he *killed my best friend*. You want me to ignore that?"

"You said yourself Tony didn't have any family. You don't even have proof. What good would it do—"

"You care about Karla and that baby. You don't want their lives ruined."

"Of course I don't."

He took his keys from her. "But my life was ruined and that's okay."

"That's not what I'm saying."

With a shake of his head, he walked around her and got back in the car. "Get in," he commanded through the open window.

She sighed but did as he asked. Without a word, they rode the rest of the way to her apartment. Neither of them moved when he parked in front of her building, occupying a space but leaving the engine on.

After an agonizing silence, Bree ran her fingers through her hair and dropped her hands into her lap. "You don't have any idea how important you are to me."

Evan stared out the front windshield, but he couldn't escape the warm gaze that filled his peripheral vision. He'd probably never hear such words from a woman again unless she were drunk or coming down from a particularly strong orgasm.

He shuddered at the thought. "Maybe I don't."

"I looked at Karla and it didn't matter anymore that Jeff cheated on me. It just mattered that she was kind and happy and a better match for him than I was. And that baby deserves a good life. I looked at her and I saw everything I want someday."

Oh, no. Not now.

He knew what she was thinking, what she would say, and it was more than he'd bargained for. He had almost considered it as well, but this latest problem proved that a shared future was not in the cards. They'd known from the beginning that they were an obvious mismatch and they had stupidly chosen to ignore that knowledge. He had to end their relationship now, before it caused either of them any more pain.

"With who, Bree? With me?"

She fidgeted. "I don't know."

He forced himself to look away from her so he couldn't see her face fall. "Do you think I'm going to fit into your picket fence world? I don't want marriage, and I don't want kids. I don't want any of it."

"I never asked you for marriage. I never asked you for anything!"

"But that's what people do when they fall in love, Bree. They make a future. We're too different to have a future. Which is why we have to stay the hell away from each other."

Chapter Sixteen

Evan wasn't kidding about staying away from her. Three days into his gig as CEO, Bree hadn't exchanged one word with him. She walked past his office more than she needed to, just to glimpse him through his window blinds. Behind her desk, she spent more time forcing back the lump in her throat than working on the website, the new brochure design, or anything else she was getting paid to do.

He hid behind his closed door nearly all day. When he did come out, he made a point to laugh and joke with the employees, usually the women, if she happened to pass by. He didn't comb his hair quite as neatly as he used to and his wardrobe included more black each time she saw him. She didn't appreciate his blatant way of showing her that their shared "something special" had come to an abrupt halt.

She hated watching him turn back into the womanizing stud she once thought he was. She knew all too well how much more there was inside him, and she missed him terribly.

Worst of all, she had no idea how to make things right.

Today, though, she planned to try. She'd found his watch lying on her bathroom sink where he had put it Saturday morning before their romp in the shower. Considering he wasn't wearing another one, he had to have noticed its absence. But he hadn't said a word, asserting once again that he had no interest in talking to her.

Too bad. It was time for bad boy Evan to act like a grown-up.

She rapped on his door, her hand threatening to back down with every knock. But she was determined to end the silence, and she didn't even wait for his answer before entering.

"Come—" He stopped short when he glanced up from a stack of paperwork and saw her standing there. "In."

Even when he acted like a jerk, he was still gorgeous. One look in those dark eyes reminded her of every moment they'd spent in his bed. Her bed. Her office...

She tossed the watch on top of the pile he'd been reading and then sat in the chair across from him. "You left that at my place."

Plucking it from his desk, he clasped it around his wrist without looking at her. "Thanks," he mumbled, as though she'd told him what the cafeteria was serving for lunch that day.

He might as well have stuck his pencil into her chest, but she fought hard not to flinch at his cold demeanor. She remained seated, her gaze adhered to his shifting eyes.

Finally, they rested on her. "Can I help you with something?"

"Knock it off, Evan. This isn't funny."

He stabbed the pencil into a cup holder. "I never said it was funny. I just don't see what else we have to talk about."

"I could think of a few things. My contract, for one. I was supposed to meet with Paula this week, but I'm guessing that's your job now. Oh, and there's also the matter of your childish attitude."

That got his attention. "Excuse me?"

"The silent treatment is for twelve-year-olds. Why don't you just tell me what the problem is?"

He crossed the room and twisted the bar on his blinds to

close them. "Bree," he said to the wall, "you just don't get it."

"What?" She rose from the chair and positioned herself in front of him so he could no longer avoid her eyes. "What don't I get?"

"I thought we had this conversation. I thought we agreed our fun was over."

"So we can't speak ever again? We're supposed to avoid each other every day? You're not even going to give me the 'let's be friends' speech?"

"Is that what you want to hear?" He held her by the elbows and pulled her to his chest, lowering his voice to a near-whisper. "I don't want to be your friend. I want to call you mine and make love to you every day, and I can't. I can't because I'm your boss. I can't because I'm incapable of getting over the fact that you slept with the guy who ran over my best friend, and I can't because we want completely different things out of life. You know that."

Yes, she knew that. Their affair was a short-term deal and she'd known that from the beginning. Now she was trying to accept that the man she'd lived with for two years had been responsible for the worst tragedy of Evan's life. And even if that weren't the case, Evan despised commitment, loathed kids, and wouldn't in this lifetime put his face on the picture of that groom she had in her head.

Despite all that, she wanted him so badly she felt it in every cell of her body. She was sure she'd crack and crumble into a million pieces if she didn't feel him against her one more time.

"Kiss me."

"Bree—"

"Please, Evan. If from now on we have to be coworkers who hardly know each other, let me have another minute with you. I want to remember," she breathed, grazing his cheek with hers.

She heard him inhale, smelled his familiar cologne as she

skimmed her face along his neck. She thought her legs would give out when he cradled her chin and drew her mouth close to his.

"Remember this," he whispered.

Their lips touched, a gentle caress that sent her every nerve ending shooting outward and made her feel like a barb-covered cactus. She pressed closer to him in an attempt to quell the sensation, but that only drove the thorns of need more deeply into her body. She recognized that feeling and knew only one thing would sate it.

"I wish I could change things," he murmured in response to her regretful whimper, kissing her neck and trailing his fingers beneath the hem of her skirt. "I wish..."

She clung to him, her knees growing weaker by the second. He found the source of her ache and rubbed his fingertips against the ceaseless throbbing. She was seconds from release, her eyes wide and her body trembling, when she caught sight of his desk and the paperwork strewn across it—documents covered with the name Todd Hartman.

She leapt away from Evan and straightened her skirt, snatched out of her passionate fog by the reality that they hadn't yet found the saboteur and until they did, her employment status was up in the air.

"What is this?" She crossed to the desk and picked up one of the sheets, her private parts balking at the abrupt loss of Evan's touch. Deciphering this mystery once and for all would be a nice salve for the pain.

He sighed. "The security log. Every time someone swipes their card to get into the office, it's recorded here. The investigators brought the information today."

Her breathing grew shallow as she scanned the list, and she put her hand on her chest. "This can't be right. Todd's been in here this much?"

Impossible. He had a family at home, things to do, places to be. He'd never spend so much time at work after hours.

"I've already called Paula. She's on her way in so we can discuss pressing charges."

"Don't you think you're jumping to conclusions?" The last remnants of her sensual mood vanished. She read the log again, scouring every word, every character on the page. There had to be an error somewhere. Todd didn't have any reason to hurt the company. Paula was one of his best friends, and he had a family to support—

"That's it," she said, pointing. "I knew there was a mistake."

Evan looked skeptical. "What is it?"

"This says he was in here last night at seven-thirty. That's not possible. His boys had a game."

Flustered, Evan thrust the paperwork back onto his desk. "Todd was not coaching baseball last night, Bree. He was at his desk. I've got surveillance video to prove it."

Her stomach flipped. "Maybe he was just working late."

But even she didn't believe that flimsy excuse. Todd never, ever put work before his sons, especially when it came to baseball. If he were at the office instead of the game, he must have had an incredibly strong reason.

But what?

Evan's cell phone rang, and he reached down to grab it from his pocket. "It's Paula," he said when he looked at the LCD. "Let me see what she wants to do. We can probably have this all taken care of by tonight."

"Wait." Bree shook her head, remembering the promise she'd made to Todd. "You can't do that."

"I'm sorry?"

The phone kept ringing, and she talked over the loud, tinny version of a rock song she didn't recognize. "There's a tournament this weekend. He can't miss it."

Evan's expression was so horrified, Bree wouldn't have been shocked to see fire spout from his ears. "You want me to let this company sink so Todd can watch a *baseball game*? That's an insult to Paula and to all the honest people who work here."

"I just want you to give it another couple of days. Just because he was here doesn't mean he was doing something wrong. I really don't think he's responsible, and you can't go ruining lives when you have nothing but circumstantial evidence."

She could tell that pissed him off, but she was tired of defending other people's families because he couldn't appreciate the value of having one. He closed his eyes like he might have been counting to ten.

"Do you have reason to believe he's innocent?" he finally asked.

"I don't have reason to believe he's guilty, and I'm not going to have him miss something that means the world to him and his kids because you can't be patient."

"I've been patient. We've all been patient, and this thing has dragged on for three weeks. We're out of time." He glanced down and cursed when the ringtone stopped. "Now, I have to call her back."

She placed her hand over his, silently imploring him to reconsider. After frowning at her for a moment, he spoke in a quiet tone. "You wanted to talk about your contract. It ends on Friday, you know."

Her mouth opened. He wouldn't dare...would he?

"Don't go there, Evan. Blackmail isn't your style."

"Blackmail has nothing to do with it. I have to do what's best for this company, which means stopping whoever is screwing with our work. Right now, all the signs point to Todd."

184

He had a point. She couldn't blame him for doing his job, but she still didn't see how Todd could be involved. "But—"

"I care about you, Bree, very much. But Paula is my sister. She's been there for me my entire life, she has more health shit going on right now than anyone should ever have to deal with, and this company means absolutely everything to her. She trusted me with this place, and I can't risk it simply on your gut feeling."

She knew where this was heading and she wished he hadn't chosen this moment to show her that he really did have the capacity for devotion to his family. It only made her want him more than she'd ever thought possible, and she was about to lose him forever.

He stood close, his dark eyes filled with sorrow. "I know Todd is your friend, and I know you admire his commitment to his wife and kids. And I truly am sorry for what I'm about to say, but as the head of this company I don't have a choice. If you insist on interfering with this lead, you're endangering the business, and I'll have to take that into consideration when your contract is up."

The statement thunked to the bottom of her gut. All she had to do was let it go. So what if the police questioned Todd? It wouldn't affect her. They might even find him innocent.

But then she imagined the fear on those boys' faces if an officer showed up at the door looking for their dad. And what if Sasha had to take them to the tournament alone, wondering if—or worse yet, believing—her husband was an embezzler?

She couldn't do it. Not without firm proof that Todd's hands had been on the brochure or in the bank account. Images of him sitting at his own desk didn't qualify as firm proof in her book.

"There's only one way to find out the truth, isn't there?" She grabbed the record from Evan's desk and hurried down the hall toward Todd's office.

"Bree!" Evan followed her, but she didn't turn around. He and Todd had suspected each other all along, and she was more than ready to end their testosterone contest.

Todd looked up, startled, when she bolted into his office. Evan was beside her in a second. He closed the door and reached for the log. "You aren't authorized to have that information."

She held it out of reach and glared at him until he understood that she didn't give a rat's behind what she was authorized to do. Then she handed the sheets to Todd.

He gave them a quick glance, then took off his glasses and rubbed his eyes. "I'm guessing you're not here to commend my work ethic."

Bree's face fell. "Are you saying this is all true? You were even here last night?"

"That's right."

Evan snorted and reached for his phone again.

"But what about the game?" she insisted.

"Sasha taped it for me."

Todd pushed his glasses back on and handed the paperwork to Bree. She took it, her head swiveling in disbelief. "But you never miss—"

"My wife doesn't want me at home. That's why I've been spending so much time here for the past couple of weeks. I'm giving her space to make a decision."

Evan's hand stopped moving, and Bree's eyes widened. "A decision about what?"

"Whether to file for divorce."

She gasped. "What? Why?"

"Yes, do tell," Evan said. "Why? Because you stole from your employer?"

186

Todd's gaze dropped to his lap. "No. Because I had an affair."

The tears that sprang to Bree's eyes when she heard Todd's confession were so rich with heartbreak, if Evan didn't know better, he'd have thought Todd had cheated on *her*.

"How could you do that?" she demanded. "*Why* would you do that?"

"I made a mistake. I'm trying as hard as I can to fix things with Sasha."

"But...you said you wanted to spend more time at home with your family. You said the two of you were doing really well—"

"My wife just recently found out, and I didn't want to tell anyone. I'm sorry, Bree. This is beyond embarrassing."

Bree's face was white enough to make her the second person in the office to pass out this week. Evan positioned himself behind her in case she did, then attempted to steer the conversation back to business before it turned into a therapy session.

"Let's try to focus here," he said. "If none of us are responsible for the sabotage, then who the hell is?"

"I'm responsible," Michelle's dejected voice answered from the doorway.

Todd rose so fast, his chair crashed into the wall behind him. "I should have known."

He mumbled obscenities at the ceiling while Michelle stood there looking miserable. Evan's head spun. He had no clue what was going on until he saw Bree carefully watching Todd and Michelle...and the look of regret that passed between them.

Oh, for God's sake.

"I never thought you could be such an ass." Bree's barely-contained anger exploded in a tone of pure disgust. "She's fifteen years younger than you!"

Evan put a hand on her shoulder and said quietly, "This probably isn't our business."

"I can't stomach this for another second."

She left so fast, he didn't have a chance of stopping her. That left him alone with Todd and Michelle, a situation less appealing than his stint scrubbing toilets at a roach-infested café to earn a few dollars. He didn't care to peek behind the scenes of his coworkers' homemade porn flicks.

The disadvantages of his executive position began to sink in. Last week, this would have been Paula's job. But today it was his, so he sucked it up and concentrated on the most pressing issue, which luckily was *not* which position these two favored.

He turned to Michelle. "Your name isn't on the log once after regular working hours. You aren't in the security videos, and you didn't sign on to your computer at any unusual time. Are you a crime-from-home type of gal, or are you protecting him?" He jabbed a finger at Todd.

"The guy that did most of the stuff is my neighbor. He's a hacker. I thought he was going to help me and I never meant for things to get so out of hand." She started crying. "But then again, I never do."

Behind his desk, Todd heaved a sigh. "I'm sure this has something to do with me."

Evan rolled his eyes. Here came his first lesson in melodrama. Soap Opera 101.

"So, you know where the money is?" he prodded.

She bunched her hair in her fists. "It's in another account. I don't have the number, but the name is Harry Ryder and I can give you his address. The police should have no problem getting it back."

He bent over Todd's desk and scribbled the name on a notepad, forced to listen to Michelle wail behind him. "I just didn't want you to think badly of me. I wanted to make up for the fact that I screwed up your marriage."

Evan faced her, ignoring the fact that she was talking to Todd. "And stealing money from Paula and messing around with our marketing would do that *how*?"

"Harry promised he could arrange it so Todd would be the main suspect, and I was going to save his job by turning Harry in. I thought that would make Sasha forgive me." She sniffed and looked at him with wet eyes. "I didn't want to break up their family. When you didn't want to go out with me, I had to find another way to prove I wouldn't be a threat to them anymore."

Jesus. This was worse than a soap opera. It was a serious case of mental disturbance, and agreeing to have a drink with her had nearly put him in the middle of it. Bree's interference had been a blessing in more ways than one.

"Well," he said, "that's all fine and good, and now if you'll excuse me, I need to make some phone calls so we can get back everything that was stolen. Might I suggest some professional help? For both of you."

"It's already here."

He looked up to see Paula in the hallway, sandwiched by the same two police officers who had questioned him a couple of weeks ago. He resisted the urge to smirk.

"Todd, you can take the afternoon off if you'd like," she said. "We'll talk later. Michelle, these men would like to have a word with you."

She crooked her finger at him. "Evan, come to my office, please."

Stepping through the maze of cops and distraught colleagues, he followed her, certain he would get an earful for falsely accusing her best friend of a felony. At least he could rest assured his job would be safe.

"I'm pretty smart, calling your office number and getting her confession on your voice mail, huh?" Of course, he had intended to record *Todd's* confession—he'd covertly pressed Paula's speed dial button when Todd had admitted to Bree that the security log was correct. But at this point, he'd have been happy if somebody's dog did it as long as things could go back to business as usual.

Paula sat down behind her desk, which was supposed to be his desk now, but since she still paid to rent the suite he moved toward the less comfortable chair.

"And I'll take credit for checking my messages when you didn't answer your phone, genius. Now have a seat and tell me if you recognize this."

His ass almost missed and landed on the floor when she held up the blue vibrator he'd thought the cleaning lady had taken home.

"If that doesn't bring back fond memories, maybe this will." Before he could say a word, she tossed a black-and-white printout into his lap, and he stared in horror at grainy photos taken from what appeared to be a webcam the night he made love with Bree in her office. "I'm sure I don't have to remind you that this is a place of business, not a motel."

He cleared his throat. "I can explain. But how did you get this stuff? Are you telling me you set up some hidden camera—"

"No. The pictures are compliments of Michelle's friend, who had more access to our computer systems than I ever thought possible. He attached them in an email that authorities were able to trace, and they should be arriving at his apartment right about now."

He blew out a breath, thankful that Bree wasn't around to witness this. She would die if she laid eyes on those pictures.

Luckily, Paula fed them into the paper shredder. "Look, Evan, you're doing a fantastic job with this place, and I really am impressed with your quick thinking about using your phone to tape the confession. But I can't in good conscience name you CEO while you're involved with a subordinate."

"We're not in a relationship." He said it too fast, too forcefully, and his heart clenched. If he thought he could dismiss his feelings for Bree that easily, he was lying not only to his sister but to himself.

Paula's gaze held compassion, but it also expressed the company-comes-first attitude that was as much a part of her as her pink hair and the infernal cancer.

"I need you to make a decision," she said softly. "If you want to keep up your thing—whatever it is—you need to either step down, or let Bree know that we won't be hiring her at this time."

Evan walked as slowly as possible down the short hallway to Bree's office, and by the time he got there he'd decided being a company president definitely had its share of crappy moments. He poked his head inside, where she was shutting down her computer.

"Can you wait a minute? We need to talk."

She glanced at him for a half-second before clicking off the power button and inspecting some dust on her monitor. "Not right now. Paula said we could go home for the day, and I need a break."

He approached her, anxious for more time with her. Now he knew how she'd felt in his office earlier, when she had asked for a parting kiss. A kiss he wished they could continue and follow on its sensual path until they reached the end and the last cries of release escaped their lips.

"I want to apologize. I screwed up. You were right about

Todd's innocence."

"Innocence?" She laughed, but the sound was far from joyful. "No, *you* were right. Love is unrealistic."

He touched her chin, searching for the hope of forever that had always been present in her eyes. "You're trashing your definition of love because Todd cheated? He's just one guy."

"One guy who had everything. You haven't met Sasha and the boys. They're fabulous. I'm not trying to be rude, but he had to be insane to get with Michelle over his wife. She's beautiful and fun, and—"

One perfect tear fell down her cheek. "You have the right idea about keeping it casual. There's no point in risking my heart when no matter what I do, he'll always find something he wants more."

"You're taking this a bit personally."

"Are you kidding?" She gathered her purse and day planner, flashing him a big and entirely false smile. "This is the best thing that could have come of this sabotage mess. I recognize now that I've got a cool job and great friends, and I don't need anything else."

She hurried out the door before he could voice the question screaming in his mind: *What about me?*

The only person who had made him believe in love no longer thought it existed.

Chapter Seventeen

The news that Evan had left PPH kept Bree awake all of Thursday night and into Friday morning. By four a.m., she had made up her mind. By eight-thirty, she'd gone through with her decision.

And now it was way past dinner time and she hadn't eaten a thing.

She hated having to quit. Paula's Pleasure House had helped her become the woman she was instead of the girl everyone else wanted her to be. She couldn't imagine waking up and going anywhere else each morning. Every other career would be tedious compared to its imaginative, fast-paced environment. She would miss Todd's bleached hair and quirky glasses, Lacy's flaming red mane and wide-open mouth.

She would miss everything about Evan.

But Paula didn't want them to work together anymore and Bree couldn't take away his lifelong dream out of a selfish desire to dress sexy. She didn't even need that anymore. She'd found the confidence Jeff had stolen when she met Karla and unexpectedly liked her. Cared for her well-being and that of her child. Realized that breaking up with Jeff hadn't been the worst thing to ever happen to her.

If anything, it had been the best. It had brought her to Evan.

He liked her the way she was. He made love to her with equal passion both when she made herself up and when she'd just rolled out of bed. He taught her how to feel, to experience, to enjoy. For that, she would be forever grateful.

But God, she would miss him.

She knew where he lived, but she didn't dare go over there. She couldn't even call him. They didn't have that kind of relationship. They'd spent most of their time working together or sleeping together, not lolling around on their own beds having heart-to-hearts over the phone.

Damn Todd, anyway, for ruining what had ended up being her last day with Evan. And for being such a horny, typical male. How could she ever hope to keep a man's attention if one would stray from a woman as lovely as Sasha?

She flopped on the sofa, and Ginger laid her head in her lap. Bree pet her and wallowed in self-pity until Jessica arrived with a hug and a half-gallon of mint chocolate chip ice cream.

"I'm so glad you could come." Bree fixed two bowls and returned to the couch, realizing how hungry she was since for the past couple of days, the pain of Evan's absence had overridden her appetite. She dug her spoon into the comforting treat.

"So, what's going on?" Mischief gleamed in Jessica's eyes. "You two got busted for banging in the office? I'm so proud of you!"

In spite of her sorrow, Bree burst out laughing. "Proud?"

"Hell, yeah. I mean, you used to be so conservative, and so scared of Evan. Now look at you. You're a porn star!"

Scared of Evan? She couldn't imagine being scared of Evan. She never felt safer than when she was in his arms.

"Was a porn star, Jess. It looks like those days are over now."

Jessica took a big bite of ice cream and shook her head. "Why's that? Sex worth repeating is hard to find. You oughta keep tabs on that boy."

"He left."

Jess looked at her, her mouth full of a second bite. "Mmm?"

"He quit. Paula didn't want us working together because Evan's my boss and he slept with me. So he quit. No notice, no nothing. He wasn't at work yesterday and he isn't coming back."

"But I thought he was dying to run his own business?"

"So did I."

Jessica set her bowl on the coffee table, her blue eyes huge. "Oh, wow. Are you telling me he left his job so you could stay? That's so romantic."

Bree chewed a lump of chocolate. *Depressing* would be a better word. What was romantic about unemployment and scarfing a gallon of ice cream? She didn't understand why Evan would give up something that big for her happiness. A tenacious man like him didn't just walk away from a CEO position for a woman he...liked. Having sex with.

Unless he felt something more.

"Oh, Jess," she groaned, throwing her head and arms across the back of the sofa. "I knew I couldn't do this casual sex thing. Why can't I be more like you? You're so good at having a good time and letting it go. Nobody's life gets screwed up."

"Are you kidding?" Jessica hugged a throw pillow. "It's only fun for so long. I wish I knew how to love like you do."

Love? Did she *love* Evan?

Jess put a finger on Bree's chin to close her open mouth. "Don't tell me you don't love him. It's obvious that you do. And it's obvious he loves you, or he wouldn't have made such a huge sacrifice."

"Jessie, don't put ideas like that in my head. Evan and I are through. We're—"

"What you're doing is wasting time. Are you going to let him go just like that? He's proven his feelings for you, whether he knows it or not. Have you done the same for him?"

No. She hadn't. He had walked out of PPH and her life, and she had merely planned to cry over it for a few days—okay, a few weeks—and then move on.

That's what people do when they fall in love, Bree. They make a future.

Panic rose from the tips of her toes to the crown of her head. Evan had fallen in love with her. He'd known it all along, all the time she'd written him off as a fling, someone who didn't know how to take a woman seriously.

He had considered their future, denying them one only when he wasn't certain he could make her happy. In the end she'd been the one to run away, because she was too busy obsessing over other couples to see what was right in front of her own face—a man who had put her needs first from day one. That kind of gift would stick around a lot longer than a diamond ring with no meaning behind it.

He had given her exactly what she'd asked for— adventurous lovemaking and the career that made her feel sexy. He probably figured she had no use for him anymore, so he had used Paula's ultimatum as a way to quietly step out of her life.

Evan downed his third cup of coffee and squinted into the computer screen with tired eyes, trying to imagine what it would be like to live in Texas, Michigan or New York. The employment search engine matched his qualifications to job listings in those states, and considering he needed a paycheck within...oh, twenty-four hours, he couldn't afford to be picky.

Paula hadn't even blinked when he'd told her he would

leave. She'd assured him she knew a couple of appropriate candidates for the job and he didn't need to worry about her or the company. Damn it, his sister could be hard-headed. It didn't matter how much they loved each other, she wouldn't treat him differently than any other employee. That was part of what made her such a great businesswoman and leader.

But the truth was, he hadn't been thinking about his role in the company when he'd had sex in the office. He hadn't even been thinking about the fact that he was *having* sex in the office.

His mind had been focused on Bree. How much he wanted to kiss her. Touch her. Taste her.

Know her.

He had done that, all of it. And when it was no longer possible for them to be together, he'd given her the only thing he had to offer—her job. The beloved career she'd sworn was all she needed.

Surprisingly, he didn't feel any pangs of regret or anger at his decision. He'd gone to school and worked for years so that someday he could call himself a company president, and there had been a time when he believed only possession of that title would make up for his destitute childhood and the brush-off of Tony's death.

But he refused to avenge his past at Bree's expense. He lived a comfortable life now, and "CEO" had become not much more than a corporate label to stick behind his name. Bree's position, though, meant much more to her than a source of income or prestige. It symbolized her happiness, her self-worth. Those were not things Evan was willing to sacrifice.

Even if it meant giving up not only his career, but the joy that filled his heart when he saw her every day.

He heard a knock on his front door and got up to answer it, hoping it was Bree and hoping it wasn't. He didn't know which would be more painful.

"Hey, stud."

He glared at Paula as she mocked his sweatpants and torn T-shirt. "What do you want?"

"I want to come in. Move over."

"Your highness." He bowed and held the door open, waving her inside with a majestic sweep of his arm.

She crossed her arms and cocked a brow at him. "I'm not the one who was messing around at work."

"I know." He closed the door, resting his forehead against it. If only his sister had a clue that for the first time in his life, he *hadn't* been messing around. He'd been more serious about Bree than he had ever been with any other woman.

"And I didn't come here to fight with you. I just thought you might want to know that Bree stopped by my office this morning. She turned down the job offer."

He snapped his head up and whirled to face her. "Don't you dare let her do that. She wants that job more than anything. She—"

"I asked her to reconsider. She refused, but I think we might be able to change her mind." Paula rooted around in her zebra-striped bag and retrieved a folded piece of paper. "You might be interested in this."

He snorted. "I don't want any more of your pictures."

She didn't answer, just resumed her in-charge stance and waited for him to open it.

Reluctantly, he snatched the paper from her and inspected its content. His eyes widened. He glanced at Paula before gawking again at the official document in his hands. "What...?"

"It's a permit. For the physical location we're opening in a few months."

"I thought you said you wouldn't be able to run a store?"

"I'm not running it. You are."

Evan blinked. He didn't answer.

"It's yours," Paula repeated. "The guys at the online office have been around for a long time, they'll be fine on their own. I'll occasionally touch base with them from home. The new store, you're in charge. It's not CEO, but it's one hell of a responsibility, and the only person you'll have to answer to is me. If you think you can handle that."

She smiled like she was Santa Claus on Christmas morning.

"Paula, um...I thought I was out. I mean, you said one of us had to leave and—"

"You're out of the main office. It's clear that you and Bree won't be able to keep your hands off each other if you're working within the same four walls."

He started to protest, but Paula stepped forward and put her hands on his shoulders. "It's also clear that you two have a thing for each other that goes beyond hanky-panky in the office. I've never seen you act so selfless, Evan. I couldn't believe it when you gave up the top position, but I figured you had your reasons. When Bree showed up this morning to leave, too, I knew what that reason was."

He shifted uncomfortably. "I didn't want to see her get hurt."

Paula grinned. "I can't punish you two for being in love. In fact, nothing would make me happier than seeing my little bro shacked up with a good woman. Just not in the middle of the office. With you in the new store, my problem is solved, and you can carry on your relationship."

Certain he had the best sister in the world, Evan hugged her until he realized he was probably crushing her petite frame. He backed up, shaking his head. "I don't know what to say."

"Say I have to leave because you need to go save the best

thing that's ever happened to you."

"That sounds good to me."

He followed her out of the apartment, and she turned when she reached her car. "Oh, and Evan, just one thing about the store."

"What's that?"

"Keep your hands off the dildos."

Bree said goodbye to Jessica, slipped on a pair of sandals, grabbed her keys and ran out of her apartment. It was dark and starting to rain, but all she could think about was getting to Evan's place as quickly as she could. She didn't know what she would say. She just knew she couldn't let him go.

She ran into a man at the top of the stairs and he grabbed her by the arms. She stiffened but before she could scream, his calm voice eased her fear.

"Bree, it's okay."

He stepped back and she looked up, directly into Evan's dark, tender gaze.

"Oh, thank goodness." She collapsed onto his chest and wrapped her arms around his waist while he ran his hands over her hair. He smelled like heaven, felt like a dream. She didn't know how she could live the rest of her life without his familiar presence filling her senses. "Please don't quit. I can find another job, this is too important to—"

"Shh. Get inside out of the rain."

They returned to her apartment, where she kicked her shoes off and pulled back her damp hair, holding on to the unsecured ponytail like a lifeline.

Evan perched on the edge of the sofa. Strands of his dark hair, wet from the rain, fell across his forehead and pointed to the always present, always irresistible silver ring she considered as much a part of him as the solemn brown eyes that watched her.

"I want you to know that I'm not going to the police about Jeff," he said. "As much as I want justice for Tony, you're right. I was acting on emotion over at the house. I don't have any proof."

She knew without asking that he'd decided to drop the issue to ease her mind. He'd lost his best friend, and still he considered her feelings. With every second, it grew more difficult to hide her emotions from him.

"Evan, I need to tell you—"

He spoke in the same moment. "And I'm not leaving PPH."

Inwardly, she celebrated his return to the company at the same time she mourned the loss of her own career. Paula must have accepted her resignation and agreed take Evan back.

Of course, that meant she would have to go.

"I'll find something else. I left my old job on pretty good terms, so maybe they'll take me back."

"You're not leaving, either."

"What?"

He rose from his seat and handed her a piece of paper he'd pulled from his pocket.

She examined it in confusion. "What's this?"

"A permit for the store Paula's opening in the fall. It's located just a few miles from the office, and it's mine. She hired me to manage it. I'll be there all day instead of at the office, but—"

"So we can both stay?"

"Yes. Just not in the same building. She thinks we'll have a problem concentrating."

Recalling the many ways they'd already had that problem, Bree crossed the room and stared out the glass doors that opened to her balcony. It was raining steadily now. The falling droplets coated the city with a sheen of moisture and washed away her anxiety about speaking her feelings to Evan. This man had given her a reason to stop running away from love. It was time she did the same for him.

He took her hand, and a glimpse of his eyes before he pulled her close revealed that mischievous twinkle she adored. "Bree, why were you sleeping with me?"

The answer came to mind immediately, and it had nothing to do with lists, or adventure, or practicing her moves for some vague notion of the perfect guy. She touched his face and smiled. "Because you're funny, smart, gorgeous, kind and caring. You make me feel like I'm in heaven every time you touch me, and you make me feel beautiful every time you look at me."

"That's quite a compliment."

"A well-deserved one."

He held her at arm's length. "I said we were too different to have a future, and I was wrong. I care about you too much to let anything get in our way."

Warmth radiated under her skin. "I was hoping you'd say that."

"Tell me what you want with me."

"I want a relationship with you outside of work. I want to talk to you and spend time with you and make love with you, because I—"

She stopped, looked to him as though for permission.

"Tell me. Let me hear you say it."

"Because I love you, Evan. I love you."

He drew her to him. "I've been in love with you since you snuck out my door and showed me that a few minutes of fun wasn't good enough. You've changed my mind, made me want things I never thought I'd care about."

Biting her lip, she gave him a naughty smile. "I can think of something you might want."

"Oh, really?"

"Wait here." She darted into her bedroom, returning seconds later with her brand new Bath Buddy. She waved it slowly in front of his face. "I'm ready for a long, hot shower."

His dark gaze narrowed and he shook his head in a mock reprimand. "You're a bad, bad girl. You know the office rules."

"I'm a paying customer, Mr. Willett. I can do whatever I want with this."

"Well. In that case…"

He peeled his shirt off and Bree followed him inside, shrieking when he picked her up and kissed her all the way into the bathroom.

About the Author

Two-time Golden Heart® finalist Avery Beck has crafted compelling fiction since age five, when she played school with her best friend and sent home a "teacher's note" that got the poor girl in trouble.

It seems natural that her two passions, writing and studying relationships, have found an outlet in romance novels. She is fascinated with exploring the "something" that draws two people together, and she hopes to share with readers the humor, fun, drama, and best of all, joy of falling in love.

Avery writes short, sexy contemporaries and believes life is not complete without the pursuit of dreams and an intense roll in the hay...or wherever one feels inclined to roll.

To learn more about Avery, please visit www.averybeck.com or send an e-mail to avery@averybeck.com.

It's not the act. It's the details...

Rockstar
© *2009 Lexi Adair*

Incredibly tight-lipped and painfully private, Anthony Phoenix has been known to make lesser women cry. Luckily, Summer Staite is by no means a lesser woman. It's her job to know his type—rich, handsome, famous and used to getting what he wants. A dangerous, seductive combination. Luckily for her it's not the man she's after. It's his story. A story that'll earn her the respect she craves—one they tell her is impossible to get.

"They" have no idea how far she'll go.

With his freight-train vocals, dark intensity and brooding good looks, Anthony is well aware he presents a challenge to the brazen columnist from Stripped Magazine. Yet she intrigues him more than he cares to admit. Beneath her soft, girl-next-door façade, she drips with the kind of sensuality that makes him edgy. High. And completely stupid.

Stupid enough to let her get into the act...and under his skin.

Available now in ebook from Samhain Publishing.

They agreed: All the fun, no messy emotions.
Until their charkas aligned…

Friends With Benefits
© 2009 Kelly Jamieson

Yoga is Kerri Harris's life, but that doesn't mean she's a New Age flake. She's a successful businesswoman, and it's about time everyone took her as seriously as her mother-of-two, "real-career" sister. That means adding a new item to her spreadsheet—marriage plan. There's only one person she trusts to help her check off this task: her best friend Mitch.

Divorce attorney Mitch MacAuley gets the cold shivers at the mere mention of matrimony. After the disasters he's witnessed from childhood, marriage equals miserable. The last thing he wants is to help Kerri down that road, but he's never been able to say no to her. He expects to feel pity for her as she goes on one disastrous date after another. The complete surprise? Thinking about Kerri with those other guys makes him crazy.

Her frustration collides with his confusion, leading to a big fight, a hot kiss and a scorching sexual tension that hits them both broadside. Prompting Kerri to propose a new plan…to add the bedroom to their list of BFF benefits.

They quickly find out there's nothing casual about the heat they generate. In fact, the burn could ruin a perfectly beautiful friendship.

Warning: This story contains a late-night booty call, hot hotel sex and naked yoga!

Available now in ebook from Samhain Publishing.

GREAT cheap FUN

Discover eBooks!

THE FASTEST WAY TO GET THE HOTTEST NAMES

Get your favorite authors on your favorite reader, long before they're out in print! Ebooks from Samhain go wherever you go, and work with whatever you carry—Palm, PDF, Mobi, and more.

Samhain publishing Ltd

WWW.SAMHAINPUBLISHING.COM